PRAISE FOR DARRELL PITT

'I found myself laughing out loud which rarely happens.'
Sondra Kerby

'An amazing book that has all the elements
of a great whodunnit.'
Ursula Sorensen

'I'm very much looking forward to reading the next book in
the series.'
Alice Hazelbaker

'This was a fun book to read. It had me laughing
a lot throughout.'
Sandy Mill

' I look forward to future installments.'
Caley Gredig

'What an awesome book!'
Michelle

BY DARRELL PITT

The Boy from Earth
Balloon Girls
A Toaster on Mars

Teen Superheroes
Book I: Diary of a Teenage Superhero
Book II: The Doomsday Device
Book III: The Battle for Earth
Book IV: The Twisted Future
Book V: Terminal Fear
Book VI: The Invisible Weapon
Book VII: The Alpha Project

Teen Superhero Bounty Hunters
Book I: Snakebite
Book II: Fear Fight
Book III: Stormfront
Book IV: Past Shadows
Book V: One Small Step

DARRELL PITT

Sun, Surf and Murder

A ROSIE RYAN COZY MYSTERY

BOOK ONE

KENT STREET PRESS

For Cleo

1

'Murder!' the voice screamed down the phone. 'Murder!

Most people probably wouldn't want to start their day like this, but I wasn't most people.

'I'm sorry,' I said. 'Who is this?'

'Edna Crayborne! There's been a murder on Rockman Street!'

Working as a journalist for the Cape Carson Gazette meant I was always on the lookout for news. Picking up the phone could produce anything, a lead story, or a whole lot of nothing. Cape Carson was so small that sometimes the nothing made it to page one.

Hopefully, this is more than that.

'Edna,' I said. 'This is Rosie Ryan. Can you tell me who's been murdered?'

'I don't know their name.'

I was standing in the Gazette's reception room. My coffee was still in hand, and I'd only taken one tiny sip of my jumbo double-shot caramel latte. The call of the coffee was strong, but I had to take things in order.

Fortunately—or unfortunately, depending on how you looked at it—I was well acquainted with Edna. She'd lived in Cape Carson her entire life and knew everyone and everything.

'Have you rung the police?' I asked.

'What do you think I am? Crazy?'

I didn't answer that question.

Edna continued. 'Of course, I rang them,' she said. 'They've done nothing! Nothing!'

'Tell me what happened.'

'I was out on a walk with Mister Smith.'

Mister Smith was Edna's three-year-old Pekinese terrier and the focus of her undying attention. I could understand her love of dogs. Trixie, my own three-year-old beagle, was my constant companion. She gave me an adoring look from her place at my feet, and I bent down to rub her head.

'And then?'

'I happened to look in the window of the old Bailey house,' Edna said. 'You know that place.'

I knew it. Everyone in Cape Carson knew the most haunted house in town. Twenty years ago, Justin Bailey had shot his wife dead in the attic before turning the weapon on himself. Even now, it remained one of the town's most talked-about tragedies.

Edna went on. 'I pass by every day when I take Mister Smith for a walk. You know what that place is like. Run down. And it just keeps getting more and more dilapidated.'

That wasn't too surprising. Haunted houses rarely looked better as time passed. Although complaints had been made to the council over the years about the house's condition, nothing was ever done. The old Bailey house just sat there looking more and more like a location for a horror film. 'And what did you see?' I asked.

'There was a blind pulled down over a window on the ground floor. It suddenly flew up, and there was a woman at the window. Her face was purple and gasping as she clawed at the glass! A man was strangling her!'

'Did you see the man?'

'The room was dark, and he was in the shadows. But I could see the woman. Her eyes were bulging, and her tongue was sticking out. It was horrible! Horrible!'

It didn't sound like the way anyone would want to start their day. Either for the person being strangled or for anyone passing by.

'What happened then?' I asked.

'The pair dropped out of sight, and I rang the police.'

'And what did they do?'

'They went into the house, but you'll never guess what they

found.'

'What?' I asked, taking the bait.

'Nothing! They came out and said there was no evidence of foul play. But I know what I saw!'

I took a long, thoughtful sip of my rapidly cooling coffee. 'I see,' I said, trying to process everything Edna had told me. She'd always been prone to exaggeration. There was the time Edna rang to say that a tidal wave had swept down her street, but it turned out to be a burst main. On another occasion, she'd said that a fire had almost destroyed her home, and it turned out to be a malfunctioning toaster that had reduced two slices of bread to charcoal.

Still, I'd never known Edna Crayborne to downright lie about anything, and that got my journalistic senses tingling. 'I suppose it was Constable Turner who attended?' I asked.

'Yes! That idiot! And that new fella.'

A new sergeant had just taken over at the Cape Carson Police Station. I hadn't met him yet. 'What's the new officer like?' I asked.

'No idea. Probably as clueless as Wilson.'

The previous head policeman had been as unlike Sherlock Holmes as I was the Queen of England. Sergeant Peter Wilson had spent as much time fishing as he had policing. The day of his retirement must have been the happiest of his life.

He had also issued no less than three defect notices to my red

2005 Jeep Wrangler. True, my passenger side mirror did have a habit of falling off as well as the horn blaring endlessly for no reason at all. I knew my car was in bad shape, but I didn't like other people pointing it out.

Sergeant Wilson had *not* been one of my favourite people.

Thanking Edna for her call, I put the phone down and took a sip of my cold coffee. At that exact moment, the door behind me opened, and Doris Glow marched in. Seventy years old and sharp as a tack, she was our receptionist and was always one of the first people into the office each day.

I'd always secretly admired her dress sense. My own grey suit combination always looked a little shabby compared to her pretty blouse and skirt.

'A murder?' she said, once she'd sat at her computer. Her keen grey eyes peered at me through her glasses. 'I've never known Edna to make things up. Unless she's finally lost it.'

I took a sip of my coffee. Edna hadn't sounded crazy, and her story had the ring of truth to it. In my gut, I knew she'd seen something.

The question was—what?

2

Doris and I were still looking at each other when the office phone rang. 'I'll chat to Harry about her,' I said to Doris as she snatched it up.

The editor of the Cape Carson Gazette is Harry Blackshore. A thin man with grey hair parted to one side, he has a long welcoming face, soft eyes and a drawl. I'd never say this to his face, but Harry always reminds me of the actor, Jimmy Stewart.

His office is the first door on the right as you head into the building. Harry was on the phone as I lingered at his door.

If you're thinking the office of the Cape Carson Gazette looks anything like a newspaper office, you'd be wrong. The building used to be a house. A sandstone building with a tin roof, it sits on a small side street off the main road. The original Gazette building was on Percy Street until it burnt down in nineteen twenty-five. Back then, moving to this new location on Kerr Street was supposed to be temporary, but the paper had operated from here ever since.

Back in the day, bedrooms in these cottages were small, and this room was made even tinier by the desk, swivel chairs and filing cabinets. The dozen piles of back issues rising like tower blocks to the ceiling didn't help either.

Ancient clippings of old Gazette stories papered the walls. Stories about the '92 storm that cut off power to the town for three days. The bushfires back in '89 that threatened to destroy Cape Carson.

And there were a few stories that weren't even local. The frontpage from the Melbourne Age when man landed on the moon. One about Nixon resigning. Another about the withdrawal of troops from the Vietnam war.

The newspaper business was different these days. It was all electronic media, and small papers like ours were lucky to keep going.

Although luck probably had little to do with it. Harry's motto is *keep it local*, and we do. We're fiercely independent too. We aren't owned by one of the major conglomerates that have gobbled up most of Australia's regional papers. The Cape Carson Gazette couldn't compete with them, so we didn't even try. We catered to people who lived in the scattered communities in this remote corner of Southern Victoria. Probably just about everyone had been featured or photographed for the paper at one time or another.

'Big news,' Harry said as he put down the phone. 'There's a woman who designs giant sunflowers from papier-mâché. It would make for a great photo-op.'

Wonderful, I thought wryly. *Paper-mâché flowers.*

I'd once had dreams of being the next Lois Lane.

Unfortunately, I never ended up as a feisty investigative reporter. Instead, I worked for twenty years as an entertainment journalist for a Melbourne newspaper before moving here five years ago. Big news back then had been interviewing some visiting overseas celebrity. Big news in Cape Carson has a whole different meaning.

My move had been instigated by my cheating ex-husband, who had decided to practice the horizontal tango with his secretary. To make matters worse, I'd walked in on them just as the tango had reached its crescendo. Some things you can't forget; that's one of them.

Harry scribbled the *paper-mâché* woman's details onto a notepad. 'I'll get onto that,' I promised. 'But I better tell you about the call I had from Edna Crayborne.'

After I told him what Edna said, Harry frowned and stroked his chin. 'I've never known Edna to make things up,' he said. 'Exaggerate? Yes. But concoct lies out of nothing? No. This bears looking into.'

'So you think someone got murdered in the old Bailey house?'

'It wouldn't be the first time.'

That was true.

'Head down to the station,' Harry said. 'And then you can contact Sandra.'

'Sandra?'

He held up the notepad. '*Paper-mâché.*'

I groaned silently.

'Great,' I said.

Taking the note, I headed down the hallway where the sound of typing came from the second door on my left. I looked in to see Ellie Applegate already at work.

The twenty-two-year-old handled our website, social media, and advertising. She was a slender young woman with dreadlocks, a nose piercing, and clear, sharp eyes. Despite me being twenty years her senior, we were good friends.

'You're an early bird,' I said.

'Catching the worm,' she replied, stifling a yawn. 'There was a problem with the website at four o'clock this morning. I got an automated alarm that the server had fallen over, and so I had to come in.'

'Don't tell me you've been here all that time.'

'I tried fixing it from home,' she said. 'I came in when that didn't work.'

She lived at a commune called Wattle Farm. I'd been there once. The people who lived there looked like hippies and deadbeats. Everyone had long hair or beards. It had taken me a while to realise that most of them were retired professors or business owners.

'You finally got it fixed?' I asked.

'I rebooted the system.'

'You mean you turned the computer on and off again?'

A smile creased the corner of her lips. 'Amazing how often that works,' she said. 'By the way, did I hear you say you were going to the cop shop?'

'I did.'

'A new sergeant's started there,' she said, giving me a look. 'He's nice.'

'Can't be worse than Wilson.'

'Ralph delivers sandwiches around there.' Ralph Eaglemont was Ellie's long-time boyfriend. Besides raising bees and growing organic food, he supplemented his income by delivering food to offices around the town. 'He's got a new standing order for a ham and salad roll. Apparently, the guy's as big as the Hulk.'

'Really?'

I wanted to ask about his height, but that would have sounded desperate. Being six-one, I hated dating men shorter than myself. I liked men who were my height or taller. For some inexplicable reason, most of the men in Cape Carson seemed to be terribly height challenged. Sighing, I wished her a good day before shuffling into the tiny office I shared with Jay Patel. He was the newbie reporter in our office and as nice a guy as you'd hope to meet. Fresh out of university, he covered sports for the Cape Carson Gazette. That, and the endless rewriting of press releases submitted by local organisations.

'Hey Rosie,' he said, glancing up from his computer. 'Is there one R in enrolment or two?'

'Doesn't spellcheck tell you?'

'Yes, but I don't trust it.'

'Good. We must be prepared for the robot uprising,' I said. 'There's one.'

I dumped my bag beside my desk before quickly checking the email on my computer. Trixie settled down next to me, and I gave her one of my homemade doggy snacks. There were a few leads for stories, but nothing that required immediate attention. I took a sip of my coffee.

'Ugg,' I said. 'That's dead cold.'

'Try to drink it when it's hot.'

Wow, I thought. *Those years of university weren't wasted.*

'Thanks, Jay,' I said. 'That's great advice.'

I picked up my handbag and headed out of the office.

3

I made my way down to Percy Street. Our town was a long way from the tourist centres like Warrnambool, Apollo Bay, and the Twelve Apostles. The tourists we got were looking for remote spots to visit or were just plain lost. Still, I didn't mind, and neither did a lot of other people in town. Cape Carson was one of the most beautiful places in Australia, and I was glad I lived here. Breaking up with George had been painful. Probably the most painful thing I'd ever been through. The one consolation was that it brought me back here.

I used to visit my grandparents in Cape Carson when I was a kid. This was where George grew up. It had been his town. In fact, his deadbeat brother, Nico, still lived here. It was on one of my holidays to Cape Carson, when I was eighteen, that I met George. It had been love at first sight. Or infatuation. Or something.

We spent the next twenty-odd years in the Melbourne sub-urb of Collingwood building a life. We got married. Had a daughter. He was a plumber. I was a journalist. It wasn't a perfect life, but it was a good life. Sometimes good is the same as perfect.

After my marriage broke up, I moved to Cape Carson with my daughter Amanda. That first year had been both wonderful and terrible. Moving in with Nan and Pop, Amanda quickly met a lovely guy named Tom and got married. That was the wonderful part. The terrible bit was when Pop—Frank Ryan to the world—died from a heart attack.

Although I'd thought living with Nan would be temporary, it had become a way of life. My parents were still in Melbourne. Despite loving them dearly, I didn't see them as much as I would have liked. And living with Nan can sometimes be...

How can I put it?

Challenging?

Still, I wouldn't want her any other way. Although Nan could be downright difficult, she was also the most supportive person I've ever known. I cast my gaze to the street. A few people sat outside cafes. Some walked along the beachfront. Despite it being autumn, a few kids were frolicking about in the water. A man and woman walked hand-in-hand along the path that followed the beach.

At one end lies the lighthouse at Carr's Promontory. At the other is Cut Rock Lookout. In between, a breakwater protects Cape Carson bay, which makes it too flat for surfers. They ride their boards around the other side of the lookout.

The police station was a street back from Percy Street on First Avenue. It was as I turned onto this that I spotted Kim Chen on the other side. She has a soft round face, short black hair, and an easy smile. She's also my best friend, though, in so many ways, we're similar and completely different. We both love movies, mystery novels, and junk food, but whereas I'm almost six-one in height, Kim's five-one. She's also a fitness fanatic. The words *fitness* and *Rosie Ryan* don't go together. My body type can best be described as hourglass, but only if your hour measures seventy-five minutes.

I can also be terribly clumsy. Giving Kim a wave resulted in me accidentally shot-putting my coffee all over the footpath.

'Oh—!'

Trixie gave an excited bark.

'Hey, you!' Kim said, crossing over. 'I didn't see you at the gym this morning.'

'I know,' I said, eyeing the puddle that used to be my caramel latte and which Trixie was now eagerly lapping up. 'That's twelve thousand days in a row.'

When would she learn that Gary's Gym was not my scene? On the one occasion I went there, I dropped a dumbbell on the owner's foot, breaking one of his toes. It was the only time Gary Carletto had ever cancelled a membership without the patron asking.

'You'll never guess who I saw there,' Kim said, as she jogged on the spot.

'Robert?'

'And Alex.'

Oh, dear. That was a double whammy. Robert was her ex-husband, and Alex was the man for whom he left Kim. They were now running an auto repair shop on Cutler Street.

'At least he didn't leave me for another woman,' Kim said, sighing. 'But I should have seen the signs. I knew he loved *The Sound of Music* too much.'

'I don't think you *can* love it too much.' I liked musicals, and *The Sound of Music* was the perfect melding of song, dance, and evil Nazis. 'That's no real sign of anything. That's how he's wired.'

'They just looked so *happy*,' she said. 'It's awfully unfair.'

'If only they'd looked miserable,' I commiserated.

Kim glanced at her watch. 'Are we still on for the movie night? And are you coming to book club this week?'

Movie night at my place was a ritual for us. Plus, we both liked reading. Maybe that's why Kim and I were such good friends.

Kim was the head librarian at the Cape Carson library.

Her specialty was local history, but she also ran the Cape Carson Mystery Book Club. Each month, a book was set to read, and we met with a few other interested locals to compare notes. Or not. I rarely got around to reading the book and just turned up for the tea and cakes.

'Movie night's still on,' I said. 'What are we reading for book club again?'

'Dummy!' Kim said, good-naturedly. '*The Murder at Grimshaw Hall.*'

'Oh, that.'

'Don't be horrible! It's a fantastic book. There are three murders by the end—and it's so romantic!'

Tears rushed to her eyes. This didn't surprise me. Kim cried at anything romantic these days. 'I'm assuming the love story was between the live people and not the dead ones,' I said, thinking, *I'd better get moving*. I needed to follow up on Edna's call. 'Anyway, I've got to go. I'm off to the cop shop.'

'Oh? Are bad boys your thing now?'

'I said the cop shop. Not the jail. I'll see you later.'

Kim said *ta ta* and jogged away in the direction of the lighthouse. Trixie and I continued to the police station, where Constable Jim Turner was staffing the front desk. Aged in his mid-twenties, Jim had a gangly build, prominent teeth, and a crooked grin. He always struck me as looking too nerdy to be a police officer. I also happened to know that he was part of a local gaming group that played a board game called *A Steam car in Dinosaur Town.*

I'd always wondered. Could someone play fantasy board

games and still be a police officer? Weren't there rules about such things? Shouldn't there *be* rules about such things?

'Constable Turner,' I said.

'Hello, Rosie,' he said. 'What can I do for you this bright morning?'

'I was wondering if you'd had a call from Edna Crayborne?'

'Oh, yes.' He frowned. 'She did contact us.'

'About a murder?'

'*Supposed* murder. Yes, Edna rang up. I went out with Sergeant Parker, but we found nothing.'

Oh dear, I thought. *So neither of you noticed a dead body lying around.*

'So what's the new sergeant like?' I asked.

'He's like me.'

The voice came from behind me, and I turned to see the man who Ellie's boyfriend had described as being like the Hulk. He wasn't wrong. Sergeant Parker was like a walking wall. He was my age, maybe a little older, and had black hair cut in an army crewcut. His face was cheekily boyish—and oddly familiar; I put that down to a passing resemblance to a young Bruce Willis.

Unable to stop myself, I glanced down at the ring finger on his left hand. No ring.

'Todd Parker,' he introduced himself and shook my hand. He had a delicate grip considering his size. Maybe he had learned restraint by breaking bricks with his bare hands. 'And you are?'

I handed him a card.

'*Rosie Ryan*,' he read. 'You're a journalist. I wouldn't have thought there'd be much to report around here.'

'Are you kidding?' I said. 'Cape Carson is a happening place.'

'Really? What's happening?'

Actually, I couldn't think of a single thing, and then noticed Todd Parker had piercing blue eyes. Guys with blue eyes have always been a personal weakness. Blue-eyed men and anything with chocolate. Those blue eyes sent my mind blank, but this time Trixie chose that moment to give a bark in greeting to Cape Carson's latest pin-up.

'What a beautiful dog,' Todd said, ruffling her head. 'And beagles are smart, too.'

I nodded, determined to keep the conversation on track. 'I'm assuming Edna Crayborne's call didn't lead you to a dead body?'

Todd gave me an amused smile. 'Not even slightly dead.'

'Edna doesn't make things up.'

'It's easy to see things that aren't there.'

'Really? Murders do happen in this town.'

'I did notice that there'd been a few,' Todd admitted. 'Sergeant Wilson must have—'

I made a *pshaw* sound. 'Sergeant Peter Wilson couldn't have found his own nose if it were signposted,' I said, glancing over at Constable Turner. 'Wouldn't you agree?'

Jim Turner was already disappearing through a rear door. 'Better file these papers,' he said. 'Should have done it...er, last week.'

Todd watched him go before turning back. 'Well,' he said. 'Somebody must have been doing the investigating.'

'You're from Melbourne?'

He nodded.

'I came from Melbourne too,' I said. 'Lovely city, but it's not like Cape Carson. We have our own way of doing things. Even the crimes can be...different. So that's why I'm wondering if you're sure that Edna imagined a murder at the old Bailey house.'

Todd hesitated. 'Constable Turner and I searched that place from top to bottom,' he said. 'There's no sign that anything happened there.'

'I hope you're right,' I said. 'Otherwise, we've got a killer on the loose.'

4

'Kim,' I said. 'I need you to help me find a dead body.'

Kim sighed. 'And you wonder why you're still single.'

'I don't wonder that at all. I know why I'm single.'

I was standing outside the office of the Cape Carson Gazette, phone in hand as the late afternoon sun beat down onto the bay. Besides the interview with the woman who made papier-mâché flowers, I'd also started on two other stories. One was about council funding cuts to a local health centre. The other was a new classroom opening at the primary school. Now that the day was over, I was finally able to follow up on the Bailey house. The police may have thought there was nothing to investigate, but I wasn't so sure.

Sighing, I stared out at the ocean. Heading south-east from here, you'd reach the island state of Tasmania, but if you went due south—and kept going—you'd eventually hit Antarctica. All that snow and ice was only five thousand kilometres away, but it was sometimes hard to believe. This was autumn and the day had turned hot and blustery.

As was often the way, a weather front was moving across the underbelly of the continent. A storm was on the way. I could feel it in my bones.

'You set very high standards,' Kim said.

'Like wanting my man to be loyal?'

'Most men are. They're not all like George.'

'So they're not all lying, cheating mongrels?'

'Not at all.' She paused. 'Although there *was* a guy who lived in town back in the sixties who turned out to be a bigamist. Or a trigamist, if there's such a thing. He was married to three women at once.'

'You're not making me think any better of men.'

'There's plenty of nice guys out there,' Kim said. 'You just need to find them. Thank goodness you've got me.'

There was something in the way she said it that worried me. 'What are you saying?' I asked. Kim was constantly trying to find me a life partner. The problem with Kim was that she didn't always think things through. 'Have you done something crazy?'

'Not crazy. Just for your own good.'

'Now you've got me *really* worried.'

'Have you heard of *Ideally Yours*?'

I had. The icon for the dating app was of two kissing lips. The company had been advertising hard across the whole south coast.

The Gazette had even run a few ads for the company.

'Yes,' I said slowly. 'But you know I don't go in for—'

'That's why someone had to take charge,' Kim said. 'You're going on a date! Isn't that exciting?'

Exciting wasn't how I'd phrase it. 'How can I go—' I stopped. 'Kim, what have you done?'

'What needed doing. I created an online profile for you, and there's been quite a lot of interest.'

Kim was telling me all this in the same way you'd say, *I cooked a sponge cake for dessert*, rather than *I've stuck my nose in where it's not wanted!* Gripping the phone tighter, I stared in dismay at the sparkling water.

'You didn't use my real name,' I said. 'Did you? I've got a reputation. A *good* reputation.'

'Of course not, silly! All the user contact information is kept behind the scenes. That way, you know you're not meeting up with an ex-con. Not unless that's what you're into.'

Oh, dear...

'That's the great thing about *Ideally Yours*,' Kim continued, oblivious to my horror. 'The app allows you to create an anonymous profile. You can even do it on behalf of other people.'

'And my username is....'

'Wow88. Turns out the other eighty-seven Wow usernames

were already taken.'

'And you chose Wow because....'

'It stands for *Woman of Words*. What do you think?'

I was thinking quite a lot at that moment. One, that I should have chosen my best friend with greater care.

'Anyway,' I said, deciding to change subjects. 'I need your help with something.' I patiently explained about Edna ringing to say she'd seen a murder at the old Bailey house. 'The police investigated but found nothing.'

'Wow. The Bailey house. It's got that secret passageway.'

'Huh?'

'You don't know about that?' she said. 'Justin Bailey had it put in when the house was built.'

Actually, I did recall hearing about a secret passage. Todd Parker probably hadn't known about it. Someone could have been killed at the house, and their body hidden out of sight.

Kim continued. 'So you want to....'

'Follow up on Edna's call,' I said. 'Investigate the Bailey house and see if we can find anything.'

'Hmm. That's right up my alley. You know my aunt was sensitive?'

'You mean she felt things keenly?'

'No. My Aunt Alice used to hold seances. She could feel the presence of spirits. She even predicted future events.'

'Does she live locally?'

'No. Aunt Alice was run down by a truck while crossing the road.' Kim was thoughtful. 'She didn't see that coming. Anyway, I'm happy to come with you. I'd love to help you find a dead body. Or a ghost. You know I've always wanted to be an investigator.'

Kim had mentioned it one or two hundred times.

'We can be like Holmes and Watson,' Kim continued. 'Or Poirot and Hastings. Or Lord Peter Wimsey and Harriet Vane.'

'So which of us is which?'

'We can take turns.'

'Fair enough.'

I arranged to meet her at the house and hung up. Before I went there, though, I needed to head home and change. My red jeep was parked up the street. Climbing in, I was quietly pleased when the engine started on its third attempt.

'Kim's still trying to get me hitched,' I told Trixie. 'Friends. Can't live with them. Can't live without them.'

Trixie barked.

My phone rang, and I put it on speaker.

'Rosie Ryan?' a voice bellowed. 'What're you doing about this dead body?'

'Edna?'

'Who else would be ringing you about dead people?'

Good point. 'I'll be there soon,' I said. 'I'm just going home to change.'

'Don't take too long. That body's not getting any fresher.'

I wasn't sure there actually was a dead body, but I promised I'd be there soon. Hanging up, I drove through town and into the surrounding hilly residential area. Nan's place was a low-slung weatherboard house with a garage beneath and verandas front and back. Nestled amongst tall eucalypts, it had glimpses through the trees of the sparkling bay.

I was just in time to see a car pulling into the driveway next door. The house was almost identical to ours, except it was yellow with an addition on the back. My daughter Amanda and her husband Tom emerged from their pristine white SUV, the words *Cape Real Estate* emblazoned across the side in a cursive red font.

They gave me a wave.

'You're home early,' I said.

'Just closed a big deal,' Amanda said.

Fortunately, Amanda's body didn't resemble mine in the slightest. She was slim and pretty with brown-black hair, and soft hazel eyes. She was also a reasonable height—five foot five—which was a miracle seeing how her father and I were over six feet.

Her husband Tom suited her well. He had literally been the boy next door when Amanda and I moved here. Tom had an eager face, and always wore a nice suit. The worst thing anyone could say about him was that he looked like a real estate agent. His talent and skills had made Cape Real Estate successful. Getting Amanda on board after she'd studied marketing at university had turned their business into a bonanza.

'Time to celebrate?' I asked.

'You bet,' Tom replied, producing a bottle of wine from his briefcase. 'Would you and Nan like to join us?'

My grandmother's real name was Nancy, but everyone called her Nan. Although she was eighty-three, she easily could have been mistaken for sixty. 'I don't think so,' I said. 'You know what Nan's like after a few wines.' She'd been known to dance on tables after a few drinks. 'Anyway, I'm following up on a story.'

I explained briefly about Edna Crayborne's call.

Amanda frowned. 'So you're visiting the most haunted house in town?' she said. 'Is that safe?'

'I'll be fine. Kim's coming with me.'

Tom's eyes sparkled. 'You know that place is sitting on prime real estate?' he said. 'A week doesn't go by when someone doesn't come into the office wanting to buy it.'

I frowned. 'People want to live there?'

'No,' Amanda said. 'They want to bulldoze it. Knock it down and throw up villas. It's one of the last remaining acre lots in town. Plus, it backs onto the bush.'

A ring of bush surrounded the town on the north side.

Having a backyard view of pristine Australian bush was obviously a draw for the place. No wonder people wanted to knock the house down and make money on it.

'The place *is* an old wreck,' I said, thoughtfully.

'Actually,' Tom said. 'Not that old. Justin Bailey built it in a gothic style, but that was only twenty years ago. No one's lived there since.'

Wishing them a goodnight, I headed inside, where I found my grandmother in the living room. Nan was always involved in some new hobby. In addition to collecting ceramic mice, she'd been doing traditional quilting for years. Recently, she'd started on her first memory quilt. These quilts used pieces of personal items like shirts and pants and socks and uniforms from a loved one. The scraps were combined to create a picture that represented the person. This memory quilt was to honour Frank.

'How's the quilt going?' I asked.

'Good,' Nan said. She was a tiny energetic woman with dyed burgundy hair. My height came from my Dad, which had come from Frank. Nan continued hand stitching a red-checked sleeve onto the scraps of fabric. 'This came from Pop's favourite shirt.'

'I remember that shirt.' Pop had worn it all the time while gardening. 'Nice to see that it'll have a new life.'

'That's the great thing about these quilts. You can create an art piece, and also use clothing and pieces that might otherwise be thrown away.' She chuckled, angling her eyes up at me. 'Talking about a new life, I've got you pegged, Rosie!'

'Huh?' I stared at her blankly. 'What have I done now?'

'*Ideally Yours*,' she said, nodding to her laptop on the coffee table. 'Wow88. Not bad—for a beginner.'

I groaned. Peering at the screen, I stared at a picture of Trixie and me. It was a nice photo; its twin was hanging in the hallway with all the other family pictures. Trixie gave a happy bark and rested her head on Nan's lap. My reaction was less positive.

'That was Kim's doing,' I sighed. 'She's determined to find me a man.'

'Good! You need all the help you can get!'

I frowned. 'Hang on,' I said. 'How did you find that site?'

'What do you think I am? Old? I was updating my profile when I found yours.'

'*What?*'

'I was updating my profile,' Nan said patiently. 'I was taking a look through to see if there was anyone else I knew, and there you were!'

'But Nan. Dating sites…'

'Aren't they great? I've had three likes and four hearts, but the guys are all geriatrics.'

Oh, dear.

'How did you set up a profile?' I asked.

She looked at me as if I'd grown a second head. 'You serious?' she said. 'You know I did that course at the community college last year.'

Nan navigated over to another page on *Ideally Yours,* and a picture of her came up on the screen. She was dressed in a short black dress, fishnet stockings and had her hair dyed pillar box red.

The photo was from the Gangster's Ball we'd attended three hair dyes ago. My eyes quickly skimmed through her details.

'Um,' I said. 'This says you're after a man seventy to eighty.'

'Yep.'

'But you're eighty-three.'

Nan shook her head sadly. 'Hon,' she said. 'I need a younger man. The older blokes can't keep up.'

I rolled my eyes and headed to my bedroom, re-emerging ten minutes later in a Pink Floyd t-shirt and blue jeans.

'Heading out already?' Nan asked.

I told her about Edna saying she'd seen a murder at the old Bailey house.

'Hmm,' Nan said. 'It's not like Edna to lie. Although she must be getting on now. Could have bats in her belfry.' Her eyes fixed on me. 'You be careful of that house. The whole place is falling to rack and ruin. It could collapse around your ears.'

'I'll be careful,' I promised as I headed for the door. 'And you be careful about who you find on that site! I don't want to hear that you're dating a hooligan.'

Nan winked. 'Who told you about Dave?'

I stared at her.

Dave?

5

'I thought you'd never get here!'

Pulling up at Twelve Rockman Street, I found Kim standing on the footpath wearing similar gear to myself: jeans and a t-shirt. We obviously had the same dress sense when it came to investigating murders.

'Sorry.' I climbed out of my jeep with Trixie happily trotting at my side. 'It took a while to get out of the house.'

Kim gave Trixie an enthusiastic pat while I told her about my conversation with Nan.

'And she wouldn't share anything more about Dave?' Kim said.

'Not a thing,' I said. 'I don't like it when she's secretive.'

She frowned. 'Who's supposed to be the responsible adult in your house?'

'Well, it's obviously not Nan!'

'Talking about men, I bumped into Ellie from your office. She said you'd met the new cop.'

'Uh, yes.'

Kim's eyes fixed on me. 'Okay,' she said. 'Spill the beans.'

Sighing, I told her about Todd Parker. 'He's tall,' I said. 'Nice looking.' I thought about how he was with Trixie. 'And likes dogs, by the look of it.'

'That's a good start,' Kim said. 'Are you into those big, bodybuilder guys?'

It had been so long since I dated someone I wasn't sure what I was into. 'I'm not sure,' I said. 'But he's already not in my good books. I told him he'd need help in this town, and he poo-pooed me.'

Kim shrugged. 'He'll learn.'

'Anyway,' I said. 'Let's get moving. We need to chat to Edna first.'

Edna's house was a clean and tidy brick home on a small plot. The lawn was cut short, and around the edges were rose and azalea bushes. Heading up the front path, we hadn't even reached the door when it was jerked open by a stick-skinny woman with short, grey hair and a frantic Pekinese terrier at her feet.

'Well!' Edna said. 'It took you long enough!'

'Hello Edna.' I introduced Kim, but she already knew her. 'Sorry I took a while. I had to get a few important jobs out of the way first.'

'Goodness! You're saying there are things more important

than investigating a murder?' The old woman glared at me. 'A woman was murdered in that house! Murdered!'

Edna pointed to the house next door. By this time, the sun was low over the bush behind the building, and the scattering of clouds had turned blood red. This only made the gothic structure seem more ominous. The building was an imposing timber place, squarish and squat. Two storeys high with a sharply pitched roof, its white paint had long since peeled like blistered skin.

Steps led to a small veranda. The roof was supported by thin rusting posts. Metal lace decorated the steeply arched windows, but this too had long since corroded red. Tiny, timber pinnacles, like claws, topped the building's gabled roof.

The once-plush gardens around the Bailey house were now an overgrown jungle of eucalypts, grevillea, and European shrubs, choked by speargrass and boxthorn. A metal fence with pointed railings surrounded the property.

I stared at the Bailey house, feeling like I'd fallen into a horror novel.

'I love it!' Kim said.

Both Edna and I turned to her. It was disturbing to see how cheerful my friend looked. Then I remembered that, while Kim loved mystery and romance, her next love was horror. Often, on movie nights, I'd peer at the screen behind clenched pillows while Kim happily chuckled as vampires and zombies took over the TV.

'It's so atmospheric!' Kim continued. 'I can almost feel an ominous vibe coming off it.'

'Maybe you're coming down with something,' Edna said. 'A cold?'

'Or leprosy?' I suggested and turned to Edna. 'Now, can you show us where you saw the woman being...er, murdered?'

Edna thumbed for us to follow. 'This way.'

After Trixie and Mister Smith had given each other a good sniffing and decided that nothing was astray, they trailed beside us as we followed Edna onto the street. The old woman pointed to the house on the other side of the Bailey property.

'Brian Ring used to live there,' she said, pointing to a 1960's bungalow. 'He died last year, and no one's moved in.'

I mentally reminded myself to tell Amanda and Tom about it. We continued past the Bailey place, almost to where Brian Ring's property met the next one along when Edna turned and pointed back.

'It was there,' she said, pointing to the ground floor.

'Where the blind is?' I said. 'You can't see into the room.'

'I couldn't either at first. Then I saw some movement. The next thing I knew, the blind flew up, and the man had his hands around the neck of the woman. It was horrible! Horrible!'

I glanced at Kim, who was almost grinning with delight. I don't know what was more awful. That a woman may have been murdered in this house or that Kim was enjoying herself so much.

'And the police checked it out?' I said to Edna.

'They went in there,' she growled. 'Came out five minutes later and said they couldn't find anything. Personally, I think they couldn't find their own—'

'We'll take a look,' I interrupted. 'Assuming we can get in.'

Kim and I made our way back to the front gate, and I told Trixie to stick close. She gave an encouraging bark. The gate was locked, but I could see from the newly disturbed rust where the cops had scrambled across. Climbing over the metal barrier, we pushed through some overgrown privet and onto a narrow, winding path. Edna passed Trixie over to me.

'The killer could still be in there,' Edna said. 'With an axe.'

'Uh, yes,' I said. 'Thanks.'

I really needed that image in my head.

Kim and I made our way up the short path to the front stone steps. Pushing the speargrass aside, we stepped onto the timber porch. The boards shifted under our weight as we crossed to the door. Kim nudged me.

'Look,' she said.

A rocking chair sat at the end of the porch.

'Yeah?' I said.

'Wouldn't it be great if that started rocking by itself?'

'Oh yes. So great. And the feeling of my hair turning white.

Wonderful.'

I was thinking that Kim was the worst person I could have brought with me. Crossing to the chair, I made out a fine layer of dust. No one had sat on it in years.

No one other than ghosts, I thought.

Just as I turned, the timber board beneath my left foot gave way.

Kra-aaack!

My foot crashed through the timber and disappeared into the darkness below. Yelling out, I dragged my leg out of the hole and peered into the gloom.

Ugh.

'Are you all right?' Kim asked, helping me to my feet.

'I'm fine. Just lucky I didn't get eaten by spiders.'

'Could be funnel webs down there,' Kim said. 'Redbacks even.'

You can always rely on Kim to bring up the subject of deadly spiders. We gingerly returned to the front door.

'I get the feeling that haunted houses aren't your thing,' Kim said.

'Whatever gave you that idea?'

Kim didn't answer as I gripped the door handle. *Locked.* Well, it obviously wouldn't be unsecured, or vandals would have destroyed the place years ago. Stooping, I peered in through a gap in the curtains and made out a gloomy interior.

I spotted an empty bookcase built into the wall, but the rest of the room was devoid of furniture. It had been emptied years ago. The wallpaper looked to be of good quality, though, and carpets lined the floor. A solitary painting still hung on the wall.

There must be a way in, I thought. If I had a rock, I could break a window. Except that would be breaking and entering, and we were already technically trespassing.

Committing another crime wasn't what I had in mind.

The cops got in, I thought. *There must be another way inside.*

A creaking came from behind. I spun about and stared in horror at the rocking chair.

It was rocking back and forth as if someone were in it!

6

Kim gripped my arm as I bit back a scream. 'Don't panic,' she said. 'I did that.'

'You—*what*?'

'I gave it a push. Just wanted to see what it looked like.'

A moment before, I'd been thinking about tossing a rock through the window. Now I was thinking about throwing Kim instead.

'Never ever do that again,' I said.

'I promise.' She gave a scout salute. 'Scout's honour.'

There was obviously no way to enter through here, so we made our way around the building.

Curtains covered the windows, but the ground floor was at waist level, so we caught glimpses of the interior. All the rooms appeared sparsely decorated and empty.

The path around the side was as overgrown as the front.

'Look,' Kim said, pointing to some crushed dandelions. 'Someone—or some*thing*—has been through here.'

'That might have been the cops.'

Kim giggled. 'This is so much like Sherlock Holmes.'

'Yeah,' I said. 'Except he knew what he was doing.'

The backyard turned out to be as overgrown as the front. I remembered Amanda saying it was one of the last remaining acre lots in town. Paths continued through a shapeless mass of camellias, hibiscus, Australian natives, and what may have once been a patch of fruit trees. A marble birdbath, covered in mould, sat forlornly in the centre. A currawong gave a lilting cry, and Trixie barked. The bird flew away.

I pointed to a framework buried beneath an overgrown bougainvillea.

'What's that?' I asked.

Pushing aside a low-lying wattle, we uncovered a swing set with two seats buried among the deep grass. It would have looked fine in its day, but now it looked depressing in the neglected garden.

'That must have belonged to the Bailey kids,' I said.

'Sad to see it sitting here,' Kim said. 'I wonder why someone hasn't moved in or demolished the place.'

'The kids are grown up now. I think they still live locally. Maybe they keep the house in memory of their parents.'

One path led all the way to the back fence. Beyond this lay the bush that embraced this side of Cape Carson. Peering through the railings, I saw a trail running all the way along the backs of the houses. It probably led to the small parking lot down the road. Returning to the house, we mounted the few steps to the back porch and tried the door. *This one's locked too.* Then Kim grabbed my arm and pointed to the window further down the veranda.

'That's ajar,' I said, crossing to it. Gripping the bottom rail, I pushed up, and it opened with a loud squeal. There were marks on the sill and on the dusty floor. 'The cops must have come this way too.'

I clambered in.

'Are you sure this is legal?' Kim asked.

'Absolutely.'

Kim reluctantly followed.

The place had all the trimmings of a gothic house: high ceilings, ornamental architraves, skirting boards, and ceiling roses. Crimson and red oriental carpets covered the floor. There were even a few paintings on the walls. The one in the front living room was of the Bailey family. It was strange that it had been left behind. The father was in a standing position with his hand on Claire's shoulder. The two kids sat on a lounge chair in front. The family looked happy, although I knew that looks could be deceiving.

We found the kitchen to be pristine but as creepy as the rest of the house. Somehow, the architect had even continued the gothic look in here. The cabinets were long and tall with decorative corners. The rose in the ceiling looked like it could have come straight from Notre Dame.

The other rooms on the ground floor were empty. All that remained of the furniture were marks on the floor where the dining table, sideboard, and other pieces had sat.

No one's ever returned to properly clear out the house, I thought. *It was abandoned.*

'This was quite a place,' I said.

'Quite a place...for a murder.'

'Remind me never to bring you on one of these again.'

We navigated through the house to the front room, where Edna saw the murder. Or whatever it was that had happened. On the other side of the curtains, there was a blind at the window. It was pulled down and made the room even darker. Turning the phone's torch on, my eyes searched the gloom for some sign of disturbance.

'Now that's strange,' I said. 'What do you see?'

Kim peered at the floor. 'Nothing.'

'That's exactly it,' I said. 'Nothing. There's no dust in here.'

She looked closer. 'You're right,' she said. 'The floor's been cleaned.'

That's weird.

A lack of dust didn't mean that someone was murdered here, but it was unusual.

The house was in remarkable condition, but dust was everywhere. Why would this room have been cleaned? And who cleaned it?

I peered down at Trixie, who was staring up at me with big eyes. Undoubtedly, her superior sense of smell was picking up all kinds of scents.

If only she could talk!

Kim examined the roll-up blind. This was the one Edna said fell while the woman was being strangled. 'There's something odd about this too,' she said, peering up at the housing. 'It doesn't quite fit the mounting bracket.'

Standing on tiptoes, she touched the top of the blind—and it toppled down with a crash! Trixie barked in surprise as I jumped. Through the window, I spotted Edna standing on the street. Her mouth fell open, and I quickly gave her a reassuring wave.

Grabbing the blind, I hooked it back in. 'You're right,' I said, once it was secured. 'There's no dust around the top, and it doesn't quite fit properly.'

'What does that mean?'

'I don't know.'

Nothing else was in here. We quickly checked the rest of the floor before pausing at the bottom of the stairs. It was getting darker by the moment, and the upstairs looked gloomy.

Kim peered up the stairs. 'Will we?' she asked.

I felt like I'd done enough investigating for one day. Still, we'd come this far and found nothing. We may as well search the rest of the place, so we started with the basement. It had been modernised at some point. Someone had transformed it into a music studio; padding covered the walls to muffle the noise. The room lay in gloom. The only light came in through a narrow casement window.

Cautiously making our way up to the first floor, we found an office, bedrooms, bathrooms, and a library empty of books. The smaller bedrooms belonged to the kids. Judging from the wallpaper, they had been teenagers, a boy and a girl. These rooms, too, had been stripped of personal belongings but still contained built-in wardrobes. The biggest room on this floor was the master bedroom, and it had a walk-in wardrobe so large you could have dressed half the country.

'Claire Bailey must have had a lot of clothing,' Kim said.

'Wasn't she an actress?' I asked. 'She did theatre work if I recall correctly.'

'I think that's how she met her husband.'

We returned to the hallway where a final set of stairs led to the attic. Exchanging glances with Kim, I paused at the bottom.

'That's where *it* happened,' she said.

'Yep. That's where it happened.'

I sighed. Some journeys, once started, have to be completed. I suppose the moment we entered the house, it was a foregone conclusion we'd visit the attic.

We headed up one flight, turned a corner, and went up a few more steps into the dusty attic. Late afternoon sunlight streamed through a single window at one end; the opposite window faced the darkening bay.

The room was far more extensive than I'd expected. Along one side were display cabinets that had once held items from theatrical shows. Some furniture still remained up here: a French chaise sofa lounge, an empty bar, and, oddly out of place, an ancient gramophone on a three-legged timber pedestal. A record sat on the gramophone: *Für Elise* by Beethoven.

We breathlessly walked the length of the attic. I peered out the window on the side facing the street. Edna was far below. Beyond lay a glorious view of the bay. Down there, a million miles away, people were heading home for the day or out to dinner or strolling hand-in-hand along the beach.

I turned to Kim. 'So where's this secret passage?' I asked.

'I've only ever had it described to me,' Kim said. 'But they said there's a button on the window frame.'

We both felt around the bay-facing window and found nothing. Trying the opposite window only took me a few seconds to feel a nub on the upper frame. Pushing down did nothing, but then I tried sliding it, and we heard a *click* from behind.

Kim grabbed my arm. 'Look!' she said, her voice rising a notch.

A section of wall had come away like a door, revealing a dark gap. I pulled it open, and we peered down at narrow winding stairs. We started down.

Kim began. 'This reminds me of that movie, *The House that Ate People*,' she said. 'Have you ever seen it?'

'No. It's on my list with *Texas Chainsaw Massacre* and a thousand other movies *I never want to see*.'

The narrow, windowless passage reminded me of an ancient mausoleum I'd entered years ago on a Paris vacation. Those stairs had led to a crypt filled with old coffins. This time there were no coffins. Just a long claustrophobic descent, our steps muffled in the narrow stairwell, and a door at the bottom, secured by a sliding latch. Pushing the latch aside, I opened the door inwards to reveal thick garden outside.

'We're around the side of the house,' Kim said.

'It's a blind spot,' I said, leaning out. 'Someone *could* have come this way.'

'I don't think so,' Kim said, pointing downwards. 'There's no indentations in the grass.'

She was right.

'So a body wasn't stored in the passageway and carried out later,' she said.

I examined the door from the outside. It just looked like a

section of wall. There was no lock. No handle. No way in, and the door could only be secured from the inside.

'No one's been this way for years,' Kim said.

I stepped back up into the passageway, we locked the door and returned to the attic. Closing the secret door, we started back across the empty room but had only taken a dozen steps when Kim grabbed my arm.

'Look!' she gasped.

I hadn't noticed the floor before. Now that I gazed down, I saw the pattern on the carpet was the stylized images of the masks of comedy and tragedy from the theatre: Melpomene and Thalia. But it wasn't these that Kim was pointing to. Two faded brown patches stained the middle.

'That's blood,' I gasped. 'The blood of Justin and Claire Bailey.'

7

It was early morning, and the sun cast glistening jewels across the bay as I took Trixie along the coastal path. This was one of my favourite walks and the time of day I loved best. Even in summer, an onshore breeze still drifted across the bay and cooled this part of the coast.

Walking was also a great way to clear my mind, and I definitely needed that after visiting the Bailey house. I'd tossed and turned all night, finally waking before seven from a terrible nightmare where I was being chased by a shadowy figure with a gun.

I stopped to peer out across the water. The wharf had only one fishing boat moored at it. The others had ventured out much earlier for their morning haul. Young people jogged along the beach. Members of the surf lifesaving club were running drills near the surf club. It wasn't even seven o'clock, and people were already frolicking in the water. The pool at the far end near the lighthouse even had people swimming laps.

I drew in a deep breath.

This is the life, I thought. *Sun, fresh air and—*

'Good morning,' the voice came from behind.

Huh?

Todd Parker came abreast. 'Getting some fresh air?'

I was about to make a cutting comment about his incredible powers of observation when my eyes angled across his body. The policeman was dressed in a t-shirt and shorts, emphasising his hulk-like physique more than ever.

My eyes shifted downwards.

'Is this your dog?' I asked.

'Absolutely,' he said. 'This is Rocko.'

His dog was a greyhound. I knew hardly anything about them, but they were sleek animals, and this one was big and grey with small, friendly eyes. Greyhounds were known for their speed, but this one's racing days were over. His right front leg was missing at the joint. I gave Rocko an affectionate ruffle around his ears.

'Nice dog,' I said.

'He was a rescue dog,' Todd explained.

Rocko and Trixie sniffed each other to check if friendship were a possibility. Judging by their pleased expressions, it looked to be in the cards. As for Todd Parker, I wasn't so sure. He seemed nice, but I was disappointed that he'd missed what seemed like obvious clues at the crime scene.

And that's how I was seeing it now: a crime scene. I was no detective, but something had happened in that ground floor room. There was no dust. The blind was askew. Maybe Edna was right. It could have been murder which meant there had to be a body, and that's what we didn't have. Someone could have moved it, although how and when they'd done that was part of the mystery.

'So you like Cape Carson?' I asked.

'It's different to Melbourne.' The man peered out across the bay. 'Back there, I was faced with a revolving door of drug addicts and pimps. No sooner did you put them away than they were back out on the streets.'

He looked like he wanted to chat, but I made a point of glancing at my watch. Besides being miffed with him, I had a full day of work ahead. 'I'd better get moving,' I said.

Wishing him good morning, I continued on the path around the bay. A solid half-hour walk, I'd done it hundreds of times over the last few years and never tired of it. Looking out at the water always gave me time to think, and that's what I was doing now. Leaving the Bailey house the night before, a comment from Edna had stuck with me.

'It must be twenty years since those murders,' she'd said. 'And that house has been haunted ever since.'

Haunted? I wasn't sure I believed in ghosts.

What I did believe in were solid news stories, and this one

had my reporter's antenna quivering with excitement. Claire and Justin Bailey's murder-suicide had been big news back then. A retrospective about the story would interest everyone. It might even make the front page.

I wasn't walking the whole way to the lighthouse this morning. I intended to turn off into town towards the office. It was just as I did this that I peered up to see a figure walking towards me.

What? That can't be…

But it was.

'Hey Rosie,' George said. 'Surprise.'

A surprise? I thought. *No.*

Surprises are when you turn up at a birthday party in your honour. Unexpectedly meeting your ex-husband when he's supposed to be living over two hundred kilometres away in Melbourne isn't a surprise. It's a shock.

'What are you doing here?' I demanded.

'I've come back,' George said.

'Just you or….'

'And Blossom.'

Right. George and Blossom. *Blossom!* What kind of weirdo names their kid Blossom?

Making matters worse, my ex-husband didn't look unhappy, although I thought he'd maybe put on a few kilos. George had always devoured anything in sight and indulged in too many beers. Still, he didn't look miserable. Did he have to return to Cape Carson looking so annoyingly content?

'Melbourne didn't work out?' I said.

'Melbourne was great, but I had problems with the boss.' He'd worked there for a big contracting firm. 'I ended up leaving.'

'So you've come back here.'

'Yep. We're staying with Nico.'

His deadbeat brother also worked as a plumber. I'd never liked him. Not only had he always drunk too much and gotten into fights at the pub, he was also a terrible plumber.

'So,' George said. 'You've been okay?'

There were a million things I wanted to say to him.

Unfortunately, despite being a *Woman of Words*, I couldn't succinctly say any of them. I tried to think of some fantastic thing that had happened in my life. Something that would make him regret having an affair and leaving me. But nothing came to mind. I hadn't won either the lottery or a Pulitzer. Life had continued on as always while he ran off to start life anew with someone who looked like Gwyneth Paltrow and was so dim-witted that I thought of her as *Pumpkin Head*.

'I've been fine,' I muttered. 'Anyway, I'd better get moving. Got to get to work.'

'Rosie, if you want—'

But I'd already turned my back on him.

I marched off resolutely—which would have looked impressive, except my foot caught on a crack in the pavement, and I almost went flying.

Swearing under my breath, I continued on to the office with Trixie close behind. By then, the steam had just about finished coming from my ears. I was angry, but there was little I could do about it. If George wanted to move back to Cape Carson, then so be it. He'd grown up here, and he could live wherever he wanted. What he did with his life was his business, just as my life was mine.

It was odd he hadn't asked about Amanda, although maybe he was already in contact with her. I rarely spoke to Amanda about her father. She'd been furious with him when she found out about the affair, but she'd cooled down since then. That was for the best. I didn't want them arguing. Amanda needed her dad. My relationship with him shouldn't affect them.

The office was empty except for Harry. The dear man worked longer hours than anyone else I knew. Somehow, he kept the place ticking on year after year, even with competition from two local radio stations and the continual assault of the internet.

I told him about my idea for a story on the Bailey house.

He leaned back in his seat. 'That's brilliant,' he said. 'We've got lots of file photos from the time of the murders. Plus, there's plenty of people associated with the house that still live around here.'

'Do the Bailey children still live in town? Although they're obviously not children anymore.'

'John and Lily? No. They run a winery up in Northville. Or she does, anyway. Cape Carson Wines. It's only twenty minutes from here. Yep, you've got to speak to them. Oh, and Wayne Price too.'

'Wayne Price?' I knew the name. He was the cook down at Sandy's Diner, the most popular eatery in town. 'How does he—'

'Wayne was the Bailey family's chef. He was there the night the murder-suicide happened.'

That's right. I'd heard he used to work for the Baileys. Wayne would be an ideal person to speak to.

'Don't forget, though,' Harry said. 'You've got other stories to cover too.'

'Uh, yeah...'

'The guy with the pizza box collection?'

I stifled a groan. 'Is that really news?'

'People love pictures,' Harry said for what must have been the millionth time. He held out his hands like a director framing a shot for a blockbuster movie. 'Think of how eye-catching it will be: the image of a man eating pizza with a hundred pizza boxes behind him. Might even make the front page.'

'Oh yes,' I said. 'Great.'

8

'Coffee!' I announced. 'And make it a triple-shot! And extra caramel!'

There were people in Sandy's Diner, but it was still early, so the morning rush had not yet arrived. I frequented a few cafes in Cape Carson—it was best to stay in contact with everyone—but Sandy's Diner was my favourite.

A few local surfer guys were outside, tucking into bacon and eggs, their eyes on the quiet bay.

I knew what their conversation would be: waves. Inside, an older couple who had obviously made the long tourist hike from *elsewhere* were hoeing into piles of pancakes.

The diner was a tribute to fifties and sixties rock and roll. Old record covers plastered the walls, as did pictures of Elvis, Roy Orbison, and other rockers. The cosy interior seated about thirty people. The red and white counter—decorated in silver trim—ran the length of one side. Black and white tiles covered the floor. Buddy Holly sang *Peggy Sue* in the background.

'Tough morning?' Sandy Clementine asked.

She was the owner and was as memorable as the place it-self. A buxom forty-year-old with short-cropped blonde hair beneath her red and white cap, she had tattoos on both her muscly arms. Those same muscled arms had once tossed out a pair of drunks one Saturday night while putting out a fire in the kitchen.

No doubt about it, Sandy was a force to be reckoned with.

'Whatever gave you that idea?' I asked, slumping onto a bar stool.

Sandy frowned as she ran the shots and heated the milk.

'The triple-shot and extra caramel was a dead giveaway.' She poured the milk into a jumbo cup. 'You know it's not even nine o'clock yet?'

'Some days, you need something extra to make it through.' I glimpsed Wayne in the kitchen. 'Mind if I chat with the best cook in town for a minute?'

Curiosity flickered across her face. 'Sure,' she said and yelled his name. 'Beautiful lady out here who wants to talk to you.'

Wayne came shuffling out. He was a heavyset black man, bald with a short grey goatee and soft, brown eyes. It was funny now that I thought about it. I came to Sandy's Diner every day, but I never thought of him in connection with the old Bailey house.

'I've always got time for beautiful women,' he said, wiping his hands on a towel.

We settled into a booth.

'Let me make a guess,' Wayne said. 'You want to talk about the Bailey place.'

'How'd you know?'

'It's twenty years since their deaths. A few people in town have been talking about it. Plus, I heard that Edna Crayborne thought she saw something at the house.'

'A lot of people have seen things over the years,' I said, sipping my coffee. *Bliss!* It was just the right combination of sugar and caffeine. 'Can you tell me what happened the night of the Baileys' deaths?'

Wayne sighed. 'It was all a long time ago,' he said, running a hand across his bald head. 'What do you know about it?'

'Only that Claire Bailey was murdered,' I said. 'It seems Justin shot her before taking his own life.'

'That's the basics of it,' Wayne agreed. 'Justin and Claire Bailey both had retired young. He'd inherited money from his father and invested it in a theatre in Melbourne: The Grange. Justin sold it at a tidy profit and moved to Cape Carson. They had plenty of money, and were still young. They had teenage kids. John was sixteen. Lily was a year younger. It seemed like they had the ideal life.'

'And you worked at the house?'

'I was the chef.' Wayne looked embarrassed. 'Mind you, while the parents enjoyed my food, the kids were spoiled brats. Justin and Claire were nice people but didn't keep as firm a rein on their kids as they should. Just let the kids do whatever they wanted. As well as me, there was Sofia, the maid, and the gardener who turned up once a week.'

'You say they *seemed* to have the ideal life.'

'Cape Carson is a quiet place, but it was even quieter back then. The Baileys had nothing to do once they got here. You need to get involved with the community to make it in a place like this. Being wealthy, they sat around soaking up the sun and surf during the day and knocking back a few drinks at night. Then they drank at lunch. It got earlier and earlier all the time.

'It took a few years, but they both eventually turned into fully-fledged alcoholics.' He shook his head at the memory. 'Then they started fighting. It was terrible to watch. Claire would throw something at Justin. He'd throw something back. It just got worse and worse.'

I gazed out the window at a boat coming into the bay. My life wasn't perfect, but it wasn't like that.

'Then there was that bird,' Wayne said.

'The bird?'

'Justin owned a white cockatoo. He'd inherited it from his father. Those birds live a long time. Up to a hundred years.'

'Wow. I hope Claire loved the bird.'

'Actually, she hated it and would always go on at Justin for owning it.'

'I get the impression they spent a lot of time in the attic.'

'They turned it into an entertainment room,' Wayne said. 'It had glimpses of the bay and the best light at any time of day. Justin kept his collection of theatre pieces there. It was like a museum. And they had a sound system. A Bose, I think. Unfortunately, the bar was there too. It got to where they just used to go up there and drink all day. Many's the time I heard the bird shrieking as Claire and Justin yelled at each other. And it was usually over nothing. Claire thought that Justin had been involved in a string of affairs. Justin thought the same of her.'

'Was any of it true?'

Wayne looked uncomfortable. 'I don't know.'

'What about that last night? The night they died?'

'I'll never forget it. There were a few people at the house that night.'

'Who was there?'

'Giuseppe Costa, for one.'

'The property developer?' The man owned properties up and down the coast. 'Why was he there?'

'Some kind of scheme that Justin had for selling off a piece of land. Meetings had been going on between the men for months. Well,' he amended, 'if you can call them meetings.

Giuseppe would turn up, and Justin would keep him waiting. Or not turn up.'

'That's a bit rude.'

'It was *very* rude. There was a lot of bad blood between them by that stage.'

There were always lots of rumours about Giuseppe and links to organised crime. Maybe they were just that: rumours. Or maybe there was more to them. All I knew is that people who crossed Giuseppe Costa usually came out second best.

'Giuseppe was waiting in the office on the first floor,' Wayne said. 'And he wasn't happy. Then there was James Nelson.'

Wayne said the name as if I should have known it. 'Wait a minute,' I said. 'The architect?'

'He designed and project managed the Bailey house. An outstanding bill needed to be paid, and James Nelson had been by a few times to settle it. He was waiting in the first-floor library.'

'I see.'

James Nelson had designed some of the most architecturally significant houses in the state. He was famous for producing great glass and metal homes in remote locations, but he had also built several faux federation and gothic properties, so designing the Bailey house would have been right up his alley.

I'd spotted him in town only once; he and I didn't travel in the same circles.

Wayne continued. 'Sofia and I were clearing up in the kitchen,' he said. 'John was there too, just hanging around like teenagers do. Lily was in her bedroom. There had been some yelling earlier in the evening, but then it had been quiet for about an hour.' He paused. 'Then, almost out of nowhere, this frenzied screaming came from the attic, and then the shots rang out.'

I swallowed. 'What happened then?'

'I went racing up there. Both James and Giuseppe were already at the bottom of the stairs leading to the attic. The kids were close behind. Sofia held them back. They were both scared. Everyone knew that something had happened. Something bad. And we were right.

'I told everyone to wait where they were while I went up the last flight alone. The attic door was locked from the inside,' he said. 'I broke it down and found them. Claire had been shot. So had Justin. He lay on the other side of the room with the gun in his hand.' Wayne swallowed. 'It's strange the details you remember. The pools of blood. Feathers everywhere. And there were two syringes.'

'Syringes? Like needles?'

'Maybe she and Justin were trying harder stuff. I don't know. But they hadn't been used. The fluid was still in them.' He shook his head. 'Anyway, it was obvious what killed Justin and Claire.'

I asked gently. 'Where had the weapon come from?'

'One of the display cases. The theatrical gun was a real weapon with real bullets.'

'So it was pretty much an open and shut case.'

'Well...almost.'

'What do you mean?'

Wayne rubbed his chin. 'There's one thing that's never been explained properly,' he said. 'And it makes no sense. The thing is....'

'What?'

'I heard three shots. So did Sofia. I'd swear to it. But Justin and Claire each died from a single gunshot. The police found no evidence that a third shot had been fired.' He shook his head. 'It's impossible, but it's true.'

'Did the kids hear three shots?'

'Lily heard three. John said it was two.'

'And Giuseppe Costa and James Nelson?'

Wayne thought. 'I'm not sure.'

'But you heard three?'

'Definitely three. There was a shot. A pause. And then two followed after that.'

'Could Justin have fired out the window?'

'The gun had only been fired twice.'

'I see.'

'Anyway,' Wayne continued. 'We called the police. Before

they arrived, though, I—well, you probably know about the secret staircase.'

I didn't want to say that Kim and I had broken into the house. 'I've heard of it,' I said carefully. 'What about it?'

'The secret staircase wasn't really a secret. The only person who didn't know about it was poor Claire. Justin showed it to me one day when he was drunk. I opened the secret door for the police, and they searched the passage.'

'And found?'

'Nothing. The door at the bottom was locked from the inside. Someone might have left that way, with Justin resecuring the door after them, but that makes no difference, anyway. It was a room locked from the inside with two people dead in it. Justin and Claire had argued, and he'd pulled a gun and shot his wife before shooting himself.'

There was still something else.

I'd interviewed enough people over the years to know when they were holding back. 'What?' I asked. 'What is it?'

'Well...' Wayne peered into my eyes. 'I've never believed that Justin did it. I know he and Claire used to argue, but it's a stretch to then go from throwing things at each other to a murder-suicide.' He let out a long breath. 'And then there's the ghost stories.'

'Oh yes, I've heard about those.'

Wayne shuddered. 'I'm not one to believe in ghosts,' he said.

'But there's been a lot of talk over the years about screams from the attic. The property's been locked up tighter than a drum for years. I know because I wander past occasionally, but that's when I've heard them.'

'Them?'

He nodded. 'Screams,' he said. 'I've heard them too—screams from the attic.'

9

'Are you feeling excited?' Kim asked.

'Huh?' I said, gripping my phone a little tighter. I was sitting at my desk and just putting the final touches on a story about a local man who had published a book about the early history of Cape Carson. I'd spent most of the day trying to put the Baileys out of my mind. Them, and the thought of the ghostly screams. 'What do you mean?'

'Your date! It's tonight!'

I groaned. 'You can't be serious,' I said. 'I can't go on a date with someone I've never met!'

'What difference does it make? You'll have a lovely time. And he's taking you to Francesca's.'

That gave me pause. Francesca's was Cape Carson's best Italian restaurant. These days my idea of fine dining was a frozen pizza and half a bottle of cheap wine. Even when I was married to George, we rarely went out to good restaurants.

'All right,' I said. 'What's the guy's name?'

'Oliver.'

'And what does he look like?'

'Nice looking. Blonde. Tall. Lovely smile.'

'Any chance of a picture? Or do I have to meet up with this ex-con sight unseen?'

She texted an image which I examined critically. It wasn't the best picture. Actually, it was blurry, but Oliver looked easy on the eye. And the picture wasn't a mugshot. That was a bonus.

'What does he do for a living?' I asked, still staring. 'He's not a butcher, is he? Or a fisherman. I mean, fishermen are probably fine, but the smell of fish—'

'Don't be silly! He's a scientist!'

A scientist? I thought. *That's different.*

I'd never dated someone *really* smart before. Most of my dates had been with guys who looked good but weren't all that bright. One of them had thought that Salma Hayek was a type of pasta. A date with someone who had an IQ over eighty could be a welcome surprise.

'Okay,' I relented. 'When am I meeting Oliver?'

Kim told me I was scheduled to meet him in front of Francesca's at seven. That gave me just enough time to get my hair done. Maybe even my nails. Providing Judy at Judy's Hair and Nails could fit me in.

I gave Kim a warning in my sternest voice. 'This guy had better not turn out to be a serial killer,' I said. 'If I end up getting killed, I'll never talk to you again!'

'Can't argue with that,' Kim said and hung up.

Sighing, I quickly sent Judy a text telling her I needed an emergency restoration.

Thankfully, her reply came back immediately: *You're so fortunate! I've just had a cancellation.* I saved my work and left the office. Everyone else was already gone. Even Harry, and he was usually the last to go.

Judy's place was a suburban house set back a few blocks from the beach. A single faded sign out the front had hung there for decades. I raced up her path and knocked.

She wrenched open the door. 'You are *so* lucky!' she said in mock admonishment. 'I just had a bride cancel right at the last moment. It turned out she didn't want to become Mrs Jabalonkowski.'

'Probably gave up because she couldn't spell the name.'

'Bad luck for her and good luck for you.'

Judy was a kindly woman who'd been doing my hair ever since I'd moved to Cape Carson. Her own locks were faded now, but she always had a splash of random colour—blue, red, orange—to lift her appearance. Lyla, her daughter, was twenty years younger and handled the nail side of things. Her hair was shaved short, and she had a myriad of earrings hanging from both ears.

The salon was in the front living room of her house. Judy sat me in her chair and viewed my hair critically.

'How long has it been since I last did your hair?' she asked. 'Should I break out the whipper snipper? Or shear you like a sheep?'

'Just try to make me look presentable,' I pleaded.

'Ah,' she said. 'A date!'

'How did you know?'

'You've got that look in your eye.'

'As long as it's not desperation.'

Laughing, Judy set to work, and the next hour passed in a flash as she worked on my locks while Lyla transformed my nails from wicked witch status to Gilda. Soon, I was racing out of there and was back at home where I found Nan working on the memory quilt. She glanced up at me.

'Somebody's got a date,' she said.

'Somebody has,' I said, laughing as I did a twirl. 'What do you think?'

'You'll look better once you've changed out of those rags into something decent.'

Growling, I headed to the bedroom and emerged half an hour later in a black dress. For the millionth time, I cursed my gawky body. Mostly, I wore matching skirts and tops, or suits. Dresses always made me look like a tent in search of tent poles.

'That's better,' Nan said, eyeing me up and down.

Soon I was driving back across town to Francesca's. It was

early evening now, and the air was warm and clear. It was twilight, and the first stars were dotting the sky. I was nervous but excited too.

This could be the start of something new.

Emerging from my car, I lingered out the front of Francesca's, hoping I'd recognise Oliver from his picture. A car drew into the car park, and I felt a sinking feeling as I saw two people emerge.

You've got to be kidding.

George and Blossom arrowed for the front door, halting as they saw me in the doorway.

'Hey Rosie,' George said.

'Hey.' I nodded to his girlfriend. 'Blossom.'

Blossom was smiling at me—which was really not all that unusual. One of the most annoying things about Blossom Taylor was that she was always smiling as if you'd just said something amusing. She wore a halter dress which accentuated her waif-like appearance. I remembered that Blossom not only did yoga and Pilates, but she was also vegan.

Her sole qualification was an Essential Oils course with a charlatan named Autumn Moonlight.

What does George see in her?

'How are you going?' she asked.

I wanted to smack the idiot smile off her face. Instead, I forced my expression into something that approximated friendliness. 'Great,' I said. 'You're here for dinner?'

'Yes,' she said. 'I've never been here before.'

Me neither, I thought. *And George never took me to places like this.*

Judging by the guilty expression on George's face, the same thought was also going through his mind.

'You're meeting someone here?' he asked.

I glanced around as an attractive blonde man stepped from a BMW and strode towards me. *Yes!* Feeling a jubilant surge of satisfaction as he approached, I flashed a jubilant grin at George and Pumpkin Head.

Oliver doesn't look much like his profile picture, I thought. *But many people don't.*

'As a matter of fact,' I said. 'I am.'

I smiled at the man. He gave me a nod and strode past into the restaurant. Another man stepped from a second vehicle that had pulled into the car park. He was very tall with silver hair and eerily reminiscent of Lurch from the Addams family.

'Rosie?' he said, approaching. 'I'm Oliver.'

I groaned internally.

Of course, you are.

10

'So,' Kim said. 'Tell me all about it.'

It was eight o'clock, and we were sitting outside Sandy's Diner facing the water. I was thoughtfully sipping on my first double-shot caramel latte for the day. Kim had insisted we meet early so I could spill all about the date. I looked out at the bay and took a deep breath. The air was cool, the sky was a clear sheet of frosted blue, and the water calm and flat.

'It would have been fantastic if I'd had the tiniest interest in meteorology,' I said.

'Meteorology?'

'That's his area of science. The whole evening was filled with him lecturing about the different cloud formations and layers of the atmosphere.'

'Oh, dear.' Kim looked disappointed. 'That's a shame.'

'He also had an annoying habit of staring at my ankles.'

Kim's jaw dropped. 'I'm sorry,' she said. 'Your...ankles?'

I shrugged. 'He has a thing for ankles.'

'Oh.'

'It wasn't the worst date that I've ever been on,' I continued. I'd once gone out with a guy who was drop-dead crazy about women in high boots. He'd spent the entire evening watching other women's legs. 'Oliver was pleasant, but just not my type.'

'I suppose things could have been worse.'

I agreed. 'At least Oliver wasn't like Randle.'

Kim rolled her eyes. 'Please don't bring up Randle.'

'I'm bringing up Randle.' Kim had set me up with several dates over the last five years, but the worst was Randle Cody. 'The man drove up and down the road on a motorcycle and did donuts on the street before stopping out the front. I thought he was there to carry out a drug deal. I didn't know he was my date.'

'You could have at least answered your door.'

'I did answer my door.'

'Yelling through the mail slot isn't answering your door.'

'Anyway,' I said. 'You'll never guess who I saw at Francesca's.'

I told her about George and Blossom. Although I hadn't spied on them, it was hard to not notice how their evening was progressing. Especially as I'd accidentally-on-purpose visited the bathroom six times, which was in that direction if you took the long way around. Their dinner had not gone well. They had obviously gotten into a disagreement. Maybe Pumpkin

Head's crystals were out of alignment, or she'd snorted too much essential oil. Anyway, she walked out with him trailing behind like a lost sheep. He glanced in my direction as they left, but I looked away.

And tried not to smile.

'Anyway,' I said, gulping down the rest of my coffee. 'I'd better get moving. I haven't done near enough walking, and these coffees are about a billion calories.' I told Kim I'd decided to follow up with John and Lily about their parents' deaths. 'Lily has a winery in Northville. I sent her an email last night, and she agreed to speak.'

'What about Edna's story?' Kim asked. 'About seeing the murder through the window?'

'I haven't forgotten, but I'm not sure what to do about it. Todd's right about one thing; it's not easy to investigate a murder when there's no evidence that anyone's been killed.'

After saying goodbye, I walked back home. There was a burst water main on my usual route, so I took a detour. I was just about to turn back onto my street when I noticed Amanda's husband, Tom, heading up a nearby side street.

That's odd, I thought. *If I didn't know better, I'd say Tom's acting suspiciously.*

I was torn between continuing home or following my journalistic instincts. The latter won out as I headed after him. He turned up another road, and I ducked behind a fence as I saw him glance back. My heart was racing as I clung to the timber palings.

What's going on here?

My stomach was churning uncomfortably. Tom and Amanda had a happy marriage. Or, at least, I thought they did. I'd thought I had a happy marriage too. Sometimes you didn't know people half as well as you thought. Staying a careful distance behind, I peeked around the corner just as a vehicle pulled over to the side of the road.

An attractive dark-haired woman in an arty flowing dress climbed out of an old Volkswagen beetle. Her face lit up as she saw Tom. She crossed to him and gripped his hands before pointing to a nearby house. The place was a rundown brick building almost hidden by overgrown bush.

Maybe this is a real estate deal.

That would have made enormous sense—except Tom had appeared so furtive. *Why is he acting so oddly?* He followed her into the building.

Tom could be there for a legitimate reason. I could bash on the door, but causing a commotion could ruin whatever deal he was brokering. He and Amanda had a solid marriage. I was sure of it. Tom was obviously madly in love with Amanda.

Or so it seemed.

My phone rang.

Oh no! I thought, staring at the screen. *Amanda!*

'Hey, Amanda,' I said. 'How are you?'

'Great mum. I was wondering if you had decided about Friday.'

Friday?

'Huh?'

'You *do* remember? My birthday?'

'Oh yes! Your birthday!' We'd discussed whether Nan and I would be cooking for the event or if everything would be catered. 'I think we might be taking the easy option.'

'Catering? Are you sure? Nan loves to cook.'

That was true, but I was finding it hard to think because I was still focused on what was going on or not going on behind the closed doors of the little brick house.

'Uh,' I said. 'We'll probably cook. How about I chat with Nan, and I'll let you know?'

'Sure,' she said. 'I'd better get going. I've got to meet Tom at the office.'

'Oh?'

'He wanted to go for a walk before heading in to finish off a settlement.'

Yes, I thought. *I'm sure.*

I hung up. I had to get moving. Lingering on the street was a sure-fire way to get people's attention, and Cape Carson was a small place.

Heading back home, I found Nan in the living room doing

her morning exercises. She did yoga with an online guru called Yogi Benthatonagi—or Yogi Ben—for short. I jumped into my jeep, drove into town, and turned onto Donovan Street, taking me inland. Thick bush filled with eucalypts, blackwood, and myrtle beech bordered this whole side of town. Putting the window down, I breathed in the aromatic smell and felt a dizzy joy. There was nothing like the Australian bush. It wasn't just the smell of eucalyptus. It was more than that. It threaded together like a mishmash of cotton and fabric at the bottom of a sewing kit.

My thoughts returned to Amanda.

No, I thought. *Tom can't be seeing someone behind her back.*

Amanda would be devastated. There had to be some other reason why Tom was seeing that woman.

Although I had no idea what that could be.

11

The bush quickly gave way to open farmland and paddocks of cattle and sheep. Old farmhouses dotted the landscape, some long-abandoned and falling to ruin. There was a shed I looked for each time I drove this way—and it never disappointed. The place was leaning so badly that I expected it to topple over.

But—no—there it was, still threatening to collapse. Still upright. When summer arrived, the heat would turn the landscape brown, but it was green and lush for now. Soon I passed another signpost on the landscape: a tiny church made of granite surrounded by a knee-high rusting fence. I had no idea what denomination it had once been. Nestled nearby, under an old wattle, lay a handful of gravestones.

Trixie stuck her head out the window and happily barked as the wind rushed past her face.

'Liking that, girl?' I asked.

She gave another bark and I gave her a doggy snack.

'Sometimes I think you know everything I say,' I said.

Trixie smiled and settled onto her seat.

The satnav on my car directed me to Cape Carson Wines. The offices and factory sat at the top of a hill. Below this, acres of vines stretched down into a shallow valley. The car park was almost full. Some looked to be Aussies from Melbourne, but there were also a few buses from which tourists were alighting. They arrowed for a building marked *Cellar Door,* beside which sat a smaller building that appeared to be an office.

It looked like a big operation.

Lily Bailey's done well for herself.

The day had turned hot. Patting sweat from my brow, I made my way into the office to see a woman I immediately recognised. I'd seen pictures of Lily and John Bailey as teenagers in the old files at work.

Lily had grown into a gorgeous woman, and the spitting image of her mother: slender, with blonde hair and an oval face. She wore a striped blue and white shirt with a logo that read Cape Carson Wines.

'Lily?' I said, introducing myself.

'Rosie,' Lily said, offering me a glass of water. 'Take a seat. You're in luck. John's dropped by today.'

'He doesn't work here?'

'John's in semi-retirement. He's made a lot of money on the stock market over the years. He doesn't come by too often, but he stores some of his belongings in one of our sheds. You can chat with him too.'

I sipped the water. 'This is a large property.'

'Sometimes I think it's too big.'

A squawk came from behind me, and I turned. A white cockatoo rested in a large cage in the corner.

'Oh,' Lily said. 'That's Spencer.'

I remembered Wayne Price talking about the bird owned by Justin and Claire. 'Is that—'

'It was Mum and Dad's bird. We inherited it after they died.' She crossed to the bird, reached through the cage, and he nuzzled his neck against her outstretched hand. 'We're old friends now.'

I looked closely at the creature. It was a strange thought. Spencer had seen what happened on the night of Justin and Claire's deaths, but couldn't tell us anything.

If only animals could talk.

The door behind me opened, and John Bailey entered. Whereas Lily resembled her mother, John Bailey looked like his dad. He was blonde, tall, and stocky with a squarish jaw. A little reminiscent of George Clooney. He wore black jeans, a white open-collared shirt, and a jacket. Lily had said he had done well out of the stock market, and he looked it.

We shook hands. 'You're doing a feature on the winery?' John said. 'I'm sure Lily will appreciate the PR. Not that she needs it.'

Lily frowned. 'Marketing's one of my roles,' she said to him. 'The business can't grow if I don't promote it.'

'What business are you in?' I asked John.

'I don't do a lot these days though I run a video-to-digital transfer business. It's more for fun. It keeps me going.'

'And John's a musician,' Lily added.

John Bailey blushed. 'I'm an *artiste* rather than a musician,' he said. 'I explore musical textures and combine them to create static environments.' He paused. 'I have a small following on *NoiseXcess*.'

Judging by his description of what he did, it was probably a *very* small following.

'Actually,' I said. 'I'm here because of the house.'

'The house?'

'The place you grew up. Where your parents died.'

John's face fell. 'Oh,' he said. 'Not that again.'

Lily cut in. 'It's twenty years since it happened,' she said. 'Rosie's interested in doing a story on their deaths.'

'Can't we just leave all that alone?'

'John,' Lily said patiently. 'People are interested.'

'I just want to get on with my life. What's past is past.'

'I can appreciate that,' I said. 'It's just that—'

John headed for the door. 'Nice meeting you, Rosie,' he said lightly. 'I've got things to do.'

Lily turned to me after he left. 'I have to apologise,' she said.

'I don't think John's been the same since Mum and Dad died.'

'I'm sorry to hear that.'

'John adored both our parents. I suppose people generally do love their parents, but their deaths struck him particularly hard. It's almost as if a light went out in him.'

I asked her about growing up in the house and the events leading up to the dreadful night.

'Well,' Lily said. 'It was terrible. They'd had a lot of arguments. You probably already know that. And they drank. No questions about that. Alcohol destroyed their lives.'

'I understand needles were found near their bodies.'

Lily sighed. 'I've heard that too, and it doesn't surprise me. They were totally out of control. Mind you, it was a complete shock when we heard the gunshots.'

'So you heard the shots?'

'I did, and I know what you're going to ask. Was it two or three shots?' She shrugged. 'These days, I'm not sure. I've always said it was three, but I don't see how that's possible. Mum and Dad died from single gunshot wounds. The police never found another bullet, and the weapon was checked. It had only been fired twice.'

I processed what she'd said. 'I'd like to do a retrospective on the murders. Go back to where it all began.' I couldn't mention that I'd already gone back to where it all began by trespassing on their property. 'Maybe even cover the stories that have circulated about the house since your parents died.'

Now Lily rolled her eyes. 'Not the ghost stories?'

'There's a lot of interest,' I said carefully. 'People say they've heard sounds coming from the house over the years.'

'The screams?' Lily looked pensive. 'Those stories drive me crazy, so I should probably say *no* to this whole thing. John and I would have happily bulldozed the house years ago, but a clause was written into the will to stop its redevelopment or sale for a hundred years after my father's death.'

'Really?' This sounded like an odd requirement. 'And the reason for that....'

'I'm not sure, but our lawyer said years later that he thought my father wanted to be remembered. Retaining the house was onc way to do that.'

'It's hard to believe it's a modern building.'

Lily nodded grimly. 'Dad couldn't have built a more haunted-looking house if he'd tried,' she said. 'But don't forget—my father made his money in the theatre. He bought The Grange, redeveloped it, and sold it for a fortune. He had a real love of shows and stage. He even did some work on the house himself. Some of the building work right at the end was completed by him.'

'Really? I didn't know that.'

'It's a shame my parents didn't stay in Melbourne. Moving to Cape Carson turned out to be the beginning of the end.'

'Do you mind if I look around the house?' I asked. 'So I can take a few pictures?'

'I suppose that's all right. It'll take me a while to find a key, but I can have it couriered to you.' Crossing to the window, she stared out at the fields of grapes. 'John was right about marketing. A news story about the house and what happened would help this business.'

'You seem to be doing well.'

'It's hard to say. Every time I think I'm getting ahead, I need to invest in a piece of equipment. And none of it is cheap. Everything costs thousands of dollars.' She looked back at me. 'I could ask John for money, but I don't want to. I'd rather do this on my own. Running the story will mean that I'm capitalising on a tragedy, but I hope you can make it more than that. I don't want a horror story about ghosts. My father was a good man. So was mum. It was a terrible combination of alcohol and boredom that brought about their deaths. I hope you'll stress that.'

'I'll do my best to give that attention.'

Thanking her, I said goodbye to both her and Spencer, and headed back out to my car. Trixie jumped into the seat beside me and stuck her head out the window as I started the engine. I looked out to see another tourist bus had just arrived. John Bailey was exiting a small building with a box in his hands. Seeing me, he gave me a short nod, and I waved back.

Trixie and I left the winery and were soon zooming past farms and rolling green hills.

'Looks like we're returning to the haunted house,' I said.

Trixie gave a less than enthusiastic bark.

'There's no need to be worried,' I said. 'A few old ghosts aren't going to scare us. Are they?'

There was no answering bark to that. Trixie simply turned back to the window, looked out at the view, and we passed the rest of the trip in silence.

12

'Have you found the body yet?'

It was the first thing I heard after I got back to the office and answered my phone.

'Uh, sorry,' I started. 'Is that Edna?'

'Of course, it's me!' Edna said. 'How many people ring you up asking about dead bodies?'

Admittedly, not many. 'A body hasn't turned up yet,' I said, settling behind my desk opposite Jay. He was frowning as he tried to edit a press release given to us by the local footy club. The club president wrote out his press releases by hand, and his writing was almost impossible to decipher. 'And just to be clear, there's no evidence that anyone was there.'

I didn't mention the lack of dust and the disturbed blind that Kim and I had discovered.

'Well, mark my word,' Edna said. 'That body will turn up.'

I wasn't sure that I'd ever heard anyone use the phrase *mark my word* outside of a British television show. 'We'll see how things pan out,' I said, deciding to match it with my own well-worn idiom. 'Anyway, I have to go. I'll get back to you if I find anything.'

'Rosie,' Jay said, glancing up from his keyboard. 'Do you think I should say lesser members of the footy team were turning up for training? Or fewer members?'

'Fewer,' I said. 'Lesser refers to nouns you can't count, like water or milk. Fewer is for countable things like slack members of the footy club who don't bother turning up for training. Which explains why Cape Carson hasn't won a regional match in three years.'

I'd only been back in the office for ten minutes but now decided I already needed another coffee. Was there a limit as to how many coffees a person could consume in a day?

No! I thought. *And I'm not addicted! I can give up any time!*

I had just turned onto Percy Street when a jogger came racing towards me. I stepped left, and they went in the same direction. Then I stepped right, and so did they.

'Oof!' I said, going down in a tangle of arms and legs as my handbag and phone went flying. Trixie gave a frenzied bark.

'Oh, sorry!' Kim apologised. 'Didn't see you there.'

We picked ourselves up, and Kim gave Trixie a pat on the head.

I frowned. 'Should you really be running in the middle of the day?' It was after lunch, and Kim was looking very red-faced. 'Didn't you do a run this morning?'

'I did, but there's no harm in a short jog.'

'You still all right for the movies tonight?'

'Absolutely.'

Movie night worked according to very specific rules. We each brought three of our own films on DVD, meaning we had six from which to pick. One was selected blindly from a bag we referred to imaginatively as the Movie Bag.

Kim mused. 'I've brought The Exorcist with me again,' she said. 'We could get lucky this time.'

'I think my idea and your idea of luck are two different things.'

A young guy jogged by at that moment. Kim arched an eyebrow. 'Better get moving,' she said. 'Later!'

I decided to drop into Amanda and Tom's office. Cape Real Estate was a tiny place sandwiched between two tourist shops. I rarely dropped in during the day, but I couldn't get the image of Tom's furtive activities out of my head.

There were a few tourists in town. Navigating around a group of teenage girls and a child bawling over a dropped ice cream, I eased open the front door to their office. Immediately inside was a waist-high desk, and beyond this, two cramped offices. There was an electronic warning bell on the door, but it seemed to have failed. From where I was standing, I could only see inside Amanda's empty office. It sounded like Tom was on the phone in the other.

'She doesn't know anything,' he was saying. 'And that's how I need to keep it.'

I frowned.

What's he saying...?

'You can't tell anyone,' he continued. 'This has got to be between us.'

I was torn between storming out or snatching up the bell from the front desk and hurling it at Tom. Before I was forced to decide, the door behind me opened, and Amanda bounded in.

'Hey mum!' she said. 'What are you doing here?'

'Oh...er, saw your lights. Just thought I'd drop in.'

The phone was hastily put down, and Tom appeared. 'Oh, hey Rosie,' he said. 'I didn't hear you come in.'

'Obviously,' I said, trying to glare at him, but I don't think he got the message. I turned to Amanda. 'Do you have a cake preference for your birthday?'

'Just make it a surprise. Anything will do.' Her eyes went glassy. 'Although I do have a weakness for your triple-layer chocolate cake.'

Weakness was probably not the right word. As a child, she'd once eaten an entire cake herself and was sick for a week. To this day, she still swore it was worth it.

'Okay,' I said. 'Triple-layer chocolate cake it is.'

Feeling more than a little worried, I headed back to work. I had lots on, and I needed to get moving. Jay was hunched over his computer, frowning as he tried to retype a press release from the surf club.

'This is not easy,' he said. 'This press release is a hundred words, and I've got to spin it out to three hundred.'

'Embellish,' I suggested. 'Just tell them how beautiful the coastline is.'

He thought for a moment before typing. 'People come from all over the world to visit Cape Carson...' he typed.

Grabbing my phone, I then rang James Nelson's number. He answered after half a dozen rings, listening in dead silence to my request for an interview.

'You know I don't often receive visitors,' the architect said. 'Especially the locals. They're not my kind of people.'

His superior attitude made my gut churn.

You're not ours either.

'There's a lot of interest in the Bailey house,' I persisted. 'Especially as it's the twentieth anniversary since the deaths of Justin and Claire Bailey.'

'But it all seems so crass,' Nelson continued. 'Mind you, I've always wondered if someone would come knocking one day.'

'Really?'

'I've got some things to say about the Bailey house.'

'What do you mean?'

He sighed. 'It'll have to be off the record,' he said. 'I don't want my name mentioned, and I value my privacy, but there are things that people don't know. It'll change the way people think about that house.'

After checking his diary, we arranged a day for me to visit. Hanging up, I wondered what the *things that people don't know* was all about. Was he referring to the secret passage? That seemed to be the worst kept secret in town. Or was it something to do with his business dealing with Justin Bailey?

My phone buzzed, and I checked it—and yelled.

'Rosie?' Jay said, looking up from his computer.

'There's a story Harry wanted me to cover! Forgot all about it!

Racing out of the office, I headed back to my car and was soon zigzagging through Cape Carson's hilly side streets. Scraping my hubcaps against the gutter, I pulled up before a tidy 1950's fibro house set back from the road. I got out of my car. The house had a neatly trimmed lawn, surrounded by grevilleas laden with red flowers. Dahlias and alyssum jammed the edges. The bees were having a field day.

Double-checking the notes I had on my phone, I hurried down the path with Trixie in tow before knocking on the door. I stepped back to wait. Anything could come bursting out at me. One person had owned seven Anatolian shepherd dogs, and I'd almost been buried under the slavering heap. Glancing about, I noticed a ginger cat dozing peacefully on the veranda. Trixie gave the cat a look before glancing up at me with a quizzical expression.

'Good girl,' I said.

A chubby, bespeckled woman with greying hair and a white dress dotted with pink flowers answered the door. She gave me a surprised look as the strains of Mario Lanza singing *Be My Love* wafted from inside the house.

'Betty?' I said. 'Betty Sawyer?'

'Yes!' the woman beamed at me. 'You must be the reporter.'

I introduced myself. The woman led me inside calling out, *Larry, the reporter's here. It's for that interview.* We entered a squarish lounge room that was crammed with bookshelves and two comfy chairs facing an old Sony television. The TV was a big black boxy thing with a graphite-coloured screen. I wasn't sure how it could even work in this era of broadband and wireless transmission.

Then I realised it was hooked up to an old VCR. A grumpy-looking man—it must have been Larry—sat in a chair, nursing a cup of tea, his eyes focused on a football game.

'AFL Grand Final,' Betty said briskly. '1997. Larry loves his football. Don't you, luv?'

Larry grunted.

'You remember who won, luv?'

Her husband grunted again.

Betty turned. 'I think Adelaide won that year,' she said in a low voice. 'Larry doesn't like Adelaide. He'll have a sniffle after the game.'

'Oh,' I said.

Watching old football games where you disliked the outcome sounded like a sure-fire way to make yourself depressed.

The crowd on the screen gave a pre-millennium cheer as Adelaide scored yet another goal. I cast my gaze around the walls, taking in a few faded prints of Australian landscapes. The bookshelves mostly held romance novels, though one had technical books. *Maybe that shelf belongs to Larry.* A door led onto the kitchen, but another looked directly onto a workroom and the reason for my visit.

'Ah,' I said, trying to keep the mood light. 'Your famous diorama must be in there.'

'Not famous yet,' Betty said. 'But it will be!'

She led me through to the workroom. A bench ran along one side with a birdcage at one end. Pairs of pliers, lengths of balsa wood, and pots of glue were scattered across the bench, along with a half-finished miniature house.

But what took pride of place was the ten-foot-long table dominating the room. As Harry back at the office had told me, Betty had spent three years building a complete reproduction of the main intersection in the heart of Cape Carson. There was the newsagent on one corner and the fish and chip shop on the other. Opposite, the road led down to the surf club, car park, and the beach. There were even replica cars.

Small figures occupied the diorama too. It was these that made the smile on my face freeze.

'Goodness,' I said, my voice rising a notch. 'Are they...rats?'

'Absolutely.'

'In clothing?' One was pushing a pram. Two were having a conversation on the street. A few were lined up outside the bank. 'That's very...interesting.'

Trixie looked worried, so I scooped her up protectively into my arms.

'I started on smaller animals first,' Betty said, oblivious to my discomfort.

'So they're...stuffed?'

'I prefer the proper term: taxidermy.' The woman pointed to the rats that had assumed the parts of humans in the diorama. 'Or even the more accurate term for my art form: *anthropomorphic taxidermy*. It involves giving our little ratty friends a new life as art pieces.'

'Oh...yes.' Swallowing, I put Trixie down and scribbled a few notes on my pad. 'Anthro...that's spelled...?'

Betty happily spelled it. 'You may recognise a few familiar faces,' she continued. 'I like to immortalise people I know, especially when I notice a similarity in our rodent friends.'

I thought that the chances of anyone in Cape Carson looking like a rat was slim, but then I noticed a scene at one end of the diorama. A rat, wearing a dress and a red sunhat, lay sprawled under the front of a model car. A group of rat people stood, posed in expressions of shock at the sight. Fake blood lay about the rat person.

'Is that Mayor Lynch?' I asked.

'It is,' Betty said, shuddering. 'A horrible woman.'

Mayor Robyn Lynch—also famously known as Mayor Lunch because of her long lunches—lay under the car's front wheels. Or, at least, her rat doppelganger did.

'And she's been hit by the car...why?'

'Horrible things happen to horrible people,' Betty said briskly.

'Oh.'

'I told Mayor Lynch that we should be allowed to preserve our loved ones after death.'

'Huh?'

'So they can stay with us.' Betty snatched up a stuffed rat and waved it in my face. 'We're allowed to preserve our furry little friends,' she said. 'Why not people?'

I gave a nervous laugh. 'Oh, yes,' I said, eyeing the exit. 'Why not?' I glanced back down at the diorama. 'Is that Simon the Butcher?'

'It is.'

'Why has he got...is that a knife in his back?'

Betty scowled. 'Accidents happen,' she said. 'Especially when you charge too much for your meat.' A cuckoo clock in the hallway chimed. 'My goodness! Look at the time! We'd better get on with this interview. My friend Mavis has a dead platypus waiting for me.'

Oh yes, I thought. *Mustn't keep that dead platypus waiting.*

Then I remembered back to the ginger cat sitting on the front veranda—so silent, so still—and the puzzled expression on Trixie's face.

Oh, dear.

13

Arriving home, I headed inside to find Nan cooking up a pot of her *pasta industriale*. At least, that's how we called it around our place. Nan was an exceptional cook, but the quantities she cooked had to be seen to be believed. There were times I thought she must have been serving when Jesus fed the five thousand. Turning as I clattered through the door, Nan told me that dinner was all sorted for Kim and me.

There was something about the way she said it that made me pause. We rarely prepared dinner this early. 'You're going out?' I asked.

'Afraid so. I've got a date.'

'Not through *Ideally Yours*?'

'Absolutely. What a great device.'

'Nan,' I said, assuming my most severe parenting voice. 'There are dangerous people around.'

'Really? I had no idea.'

I tried speaking further to her, but Nan airily batted away

my objections as she headed off to her bedroom to get changed. Meanwhile, I got a text message from Kim telling me she was bringing food.

Don't bring too much, I texted back. *We'll have enough to feed the entire town.*

She'd ignore me—she always did—so I took Trixie for a walk. Anything to battle the upcoming assault of calories. I marched resolutely from our place and headed down to the bush at the end of our street.

The well-worn path from here led to Cut Rock lookout. Trixie went racing ahead while I trailed behind. *I need to get more exercise.* The first part was uphill, and I was puffing by the time the ground evened out, and the bush closed in around me. It was quiet up here but not deserted. A woman aged around seventy with short-cropped grey hair went jogging past.

Show off!

The trail inclined upwards again, and I caught glimpses through the foliage of the town and the ocean beyond.

I was huffing by the time I reached the car park. Beyond it lay the lookout, through which a colossal crack ran through the middle. Six feet across at the entry, it narrowed to a point thirty feet inland. Far below came the whoosh of waves as they swept into the rocky wall in the huge cleft. A retaining fence ran the whole length of the lookout. Leaning on this, I wiped away sweat as a few stray drops of cool ocean vapour were carried upwards, cooling my face.

That feels good.

Staring down into the abyss fifty feet below, I saw a mash of black rocks, foam, seaweed, and dark water. The waves surged and crashed into the crack, sending another volley of vapour into the air.

A few people stood near the edge, looking out to sea. I wandered over and stared out at the endless shifting water. It was calm and had turned a shimmering deep blue. The sky above was slowly darkening with high cloud smeared grey and pink. A seagull flew overhead, coasting upwards on a gentle breeze.

I'd seen this view hundreds of times and never tired of it.

Trixie barked and was accompanied by another woofy greeting. Glancing down, I saw a familiar three-legged greyhound. Behind Rocko stood the hulking form of Todd Parker.

'G'day, Rosie.'

'Sergeant Parker.'

'Please call me Todd.'

I nodded to the ocean. 'Enjoying the view?'

'It's a beautiful sight.'

'Anything's nice after Melbourne.'

I'd lived in Cape Carson long enough to develop an aversion to big cities. Mind you, Melbourne was a great city, but it was still a city. There was something special about living in an area where it's not quite like *Cheers*—where everyone knows your name—but it's similar. Familiar streets don't make a life; it's familiar people who do that.

'There was always lots to see and do in Melbourne,' Todd said. 'It's a good town.'

'If it's so good, why did you move here?'

'You know what they say. A change is as good as a holiday.'

Sure, I know that saying, I thought. *And it's a lovely way to neatly sidestep a question.*

He glanced back towards the ravine. 'That's quite a drop,' he said as another whoosh erupted. 'Good thing they've got that retaining fence.'

'Some people still ignore it, though,' I said. 'People have been known to jump across.'

'Jump? That's crazy. The widest point is about six feet, and you can't get a run-up because of the fence.'

'It *is* dangerous. You'd never catch me doing it.' Now seemed a good time to change the conversation. 'I don't suppose there's any movement on the murder at the Bailey house.'

Todd raised an eyebrow. 'No one's been killed at the Bailey house,' he said. 'Barring what happened years ago.'

I thought about the disturbed blind and the missing dust. Turning, I gazed out at the ocean. 'That's a beautiful sailing ship out there,' I said, pointing. 'What is it? A sloop?'

He gazed out. 'Looks like it.'

The quiet of Cut Rock was broken by the roar of a vehicle as it came chugging up the hill. I quietly *tut-tutted* as it reached the car park. It was not only loud in terms of noise but also in appearance. The 1970's Valiant had been hotted up. The ebony black body had purple and gold flames running down both sides. A red and black star had been painted on the hub caps.

I peered at the driver. He was no spring chicken, seventy if he was a day.

Goodness, I thought. *Isn't he too old for that sort of thing?*

My gaze settled on his passenger.

Huh?

'*Nan?*' I said, stumbling over to the passenger side. 'What on Earth—'

'Rosie,' Nan said, grinning. 'I thought I might see you up here.'

'What are you...who...why....'

'This is Dave,' Nan said. 'We're going for a drive.'

'Pleased to meet you,' Dave said, smiling affably as he reached over to shake my numb hand. His grey hair was cut into a crewcut. He had a neat, boxed beard. A gold earring hung from one ear. Tattoos ran up both arms. One faded image read *Wild Child*. 'You must be Rosie.'

'Yes...I'm she...her....' I turned to Nan, who was delighting in my discomfort.

'And who's this?' Nan asked.

I'd lost the power of speech, which meant that Todd Parker had to introduce himself.

'So you're our new police officer?' Nan said.

'I am, indeed.'

'Did Rosie tell you we do things a little differently down here?'

Todd gave me a sideways glance. 'She mentioned that.'

'Did you know she's single?'

Before Todd could answer, I grabbed Nan's arm. 'Nan?' I said. 'Can we have a word?'

Todd Parker took this opportunity to make good his escape. 'Nice seeing you again,' he said to me before turning to Nan and Dave. 'Love the car. It's real...subtle.'

Heading off, Rocko and Trixie gave each other a farewell bark as I dragged Nan away a short distance.

'Are you crazy?' I asked. 'You can't be seen in that thing!'

'Why not?'

'It's...it's...' I couldn't think of a single good reason. 'But what will people think?'

'Who cares?' Nan gently touched my arm. 'And neither should you.'

'But the car...the man....' I stopped. 'What about Pop?'

'Rosie,' Nan said gently. 'I loved Frank dearly. I still do. But you know the best thing about love? It's limitless. It's possible to love more than one person at a time. And your grandfather would want me to live life. I know that for a fact.'

There was obviously nothing I could say to that. 'Okay,' I said, then pointed to the car. 'But *this*?'

'I know,' Nan said, unsuccessfully stifling a grin. '*So* hot.'

Groaning, I gave up. 'Just be careful.'

'Always am.'

We headed back to the car, Nan climbed in, and Dave restarted the engine. She leaned out the window. 'You know the most dangerous part,' she said, winking. 'Dave's a younger man. Only seventy-seven. *Anything* could happen!'

And with that, they roared down the hill and disappeared from sight.

14

'Okay,' I said. 'We have a winner—and it's *Key Largo*!'

Kim sighed. 'Looks like we miss out on *Attack of the Face Eaters* for another week.'

'Yeah,' I said. 'Tragic.'

We'd already had bowls of Nan's pasta, and it was delicious as usual. Age had not diminished her cooking skills. Now we settled down with popcorn and diet drinks to watch the film. I'd seen it once before but forgotten how good it was. As the story progressed, and the storm grew worse in the movie, so the weather changed outside. It started raining and only grew stronger as the evening passed. By the time the movie drew to a close, a full-blown tempest was raging outside.

Just as the end-credits rolled, the sound of a revving engine came from the street. Kim and I crowded around the front door as Dave's car pulled up. Nan and Dave climbed out, and Dave threw up an umbrella to shelter Nan from the rain. Laughing, they started up the front path.

'Looks like Nan had a nice time,' Kim said. 'You know, I heard they can do quickie weddings in Warrnambool.'

'I hate you.'

Laughing, Kim wished me goodnight and headed off as Dave delivered Nan to the front door. He gave Nan a tiny peck on the cheek before heading back to his car.

'Well?' I said to Nan.

'Well—what?'

'Do you know what time it is?'

Before she could answer, Dave's car horn delivered a singsong chorus, and he roared down the street.

'I didn't notice,' Nan said. 'Did you have a nice evening?'

I could tell that Nan would say nothing more. The following day, she was no better when I quizzed her at breakfast. Her only reply was *Somebody's got to paint the town red*. Rolling my eyes, I gave up and took Trixie for a walk. The storm from the previous night had passed, but the weather had stayed cold and the skies grey. We hadn't gone far when I met Kim on her morning run. She quizzed me about Nan's evening out, laughing when I told her about Nan's silence.

'She *is* a grown woman, you know,' Kim said, still jogging on the spot. 'She can make her own decisions.'

Grumbling, I agreed. 'I just don't want to see her get hurt.'

'It depends on what her expectations are. Anyway, you know how tough she can be.'

Nan did have a reputation for toughness. She'd once fought off a mugger on the main street of Cape Carson with a handbag.

Kim asked if I was still investigating the old Bailey house.

'Absolutely,' I said. 'Lily Bailey said she was sending me the key.' I looked at her hopefully. 'Don't suppose you feel like joining me?'

'Are you kidding?' she said. 'I wouldn't miss another tour of the most haunted house in town for anything.'

'You're completely weird.'

'And that's why you love me.'

I said I'd text her later to arrange a time. Heading back home, I got ready for work and was soon in the office putting the final touches on my story about Betty Sawyer's diorama. Jay had come in by then, and I sent him the pictures I'd taken.

'These are hilarious,' he said.

'I'm still trying to come up with a headline.'

'How about *Rats To You!*'

Laughing, I said I'd run it by Harry. Half an hour later, a courier arrived, and with it the key to the Bailey house. I rang Kim, and I was soon meeting her back at the property. The rain began again as Kim and I huddled together under an umbrella on the footpath outside.

There was no way the place would look any more cheerful on a cold and blustery day—and it didn't.

'Wow,' Kim said, peering up at the old place. 'All we need now is a ghostly figure at a window.'

'Great. That should bring on my first heart attack. A screaming demon from Hell would be a nice touch too.'

'I don't think that's likely. But you never know—'

Ignoring her, I unlocked the front gate, and we followed the overgrown path to the front veranda. By then, the rain had begun in earnest. Inserting the key into the front door lock, it was with a sense of relief that it swung open.

Kim leaned in. 'Still feels like home.'

'As long as you live with the Addams Family.'

A groan of thunder pressed against my eardrums, and the rain fell even harder as I slammed the door behind us. The rain turned to distant static. We did another methodical search of the place, our feet clattering on the floorboards as we moved about the building. This time I took plenty of photos for the story.

We were in the master bedroom when Kim pointed to the floor.

'What's that?' she said.

I peered down. At first, I saw nothing. Then, I realised some coloured paper was poking out from under the skirting board. I snatched it up: a pamphlet.

'Seaview Lodge,' I read.

'That rundown dive on Dixon street? I had a friend who

stayed there once. She got bedbugs.'

'How can this be here?' I said, looking up.

'It must have been dropped by the killer! Or the victim!'

'Let's not jump to conclusions,' I said. 'It could have also been Sergeant Parker, although I can't see any reason why he'd be carrying this about.'

'We need to visit that hotel.'

I agreed. But first, we rechecked the rest of the house. Kim fell silent when we saw the stains on the attic floor again. She may have loved horror but seeing the true-life version of it differed from the movies.

We made our way down the secret passage. The ground outside the exit was still undisturbed. *No one's come this way.* Returning to the attic, we were about to leave when Kim frowned and pointed to one corner.

'Look over there,' she said, indicating what I'd taken to be a dust bunny.

I took a closer look. 'They're feathers,' I said. 'They must belong to Spencer.'

'Spencer?'

'Their bird.'

I explained on the way back to the car. It only took a few minutes to reach the Seaview Hotel, and I could immediately see why I'd never been before. If Wikipedia needed a photo of something to represent seedy, they need look no further. Back in the 1950s, when it was built, the Seaview might have been a classy place—but I doubted it. Back then, I suspected it looked cheap and nasty, and time had only enhanced this image.

It was a single-storey fibro and brick place with a cracked trapezoid-shaped sign with the hotel's name.

Cheap aluminium windows faced the street with chocolate brown doors interspersed between them. At least two of the doors had been patched up over the years: it looked like someone had tried kicking them in, probably during some long-forgotten Saturday night rampage.

The only difference in the architecture was the office at one end. The window here was larger so the owner could look out onto the car park. Right now, the car park was almost empty. I wasn't sure if that was because the place was such a dive or because the guests had escaped for the day. Anything to get out of the hotel!

'So,' Kim said. 'What now?'

'Now we ask some questions,' I said.

We made our way to the office, where a prune-faced woman sat behind a desk. A calendar, three years old, decorated the wall behind her, and a printed quote that read, *You don't tell me your problems, I won't tell you mine.* At the end of the counter, a small TV was playing a morning soap opera.

The computer monitor was probably supposed to display a booking system. Instead, it seemed we'd interrupted the woman's early morning round of online poker.

It was hard to breathe in the office. Part of it was the cigarette smouldering in the ashtray, but it was more the accumulated smell of a million cigarettes over decades.

The woman gave us something that approximated a smile, but this quickly evaporated when I told her I was a journalist with the Cape Carson Gazette.

'And who are you?' she asked Kim.

'My photographer,' I said.

'Where's her camera?'

Kim held up her phone.

The woman grunted. 'Is this about the garbage again?' she asked. 'We can't help that people put unsavoury things into the rubbish.'

My mind went back several months. I'd forgotten that we had run a story about this place. Something about...

'The inflatable goat!' Kim said.

Oh yes. That was it. As a garbage truck had come around to empty the rubbish, a blow-up goat had bounced free of the trash and ended up in someone's front yard. The photo was so odd that it made the front page. Apparently, this was the place of choice for bachelor's parties. Reputable hotels didn't allow such events.

'This time, I'm not here about rubbish,' I said, hoping she would take the hint that I might come back again. People only want to see journalists when it makes them look good. 'I'm wondering if you've had any unusual guests staying here.'

'Unusual?' she said.

That was probably a silly question. Anyone who stayed here was unusual or unwise.

'Anyone odd?' I asked.

The woman frowned and took a long pull of her cigarette. The smoke escaped through her nostrils like two wispy snakes. 'There's the woman in room six,' she said.

'What about her?' I asked.

'She booked a week in advance, but I haven't seen her in days.'

'Is her car here?'

'It's the Kia parked out there.' The woman pointed to a battered sedan with her cigarette. 'Hope I don't have to get it towed. Did that for a guy who died from a heart attack.' She shook her head. 'More trouble than it's worth.'

I wondered if she meant the towing or the man dying from the heart attack.

'I don't suppose we can take a look in the room?'

'No can do. I did that once and almost got fired.'

Thanking the woman, we headed off and walked past the hotel rooms to number six. The curtain was pulled shut, so it was impossible to see inside.

'What are we going to do?' Kim asked.

I was stuck. 'There's the legal option,' I said. 'Then there's the other option.'

'The illegal option?'

'Yep.'

'Why not just call it that?'

'Well...'

15

Unit six's window was covered with a gauze curtain; it was impossible to see inside. Continuing along the length of the apartments, we passed an open door where a weighty man sat in the doorway sipping a glass of beer. He nodded as if this were the most natural thing in the world to be doing in the middle of the morning. Continuing to the end of the building, we turned the corner and proceeded around the back.

I swallowed hard as I scanned the minefield. If the front of the place looked terrible, the rear looked even worse. The grass was long and filled with scraps of paper, old Coke cans, and railway sleepers. Snakes loved long grass and pieces of timber. I envisioned the front page of the Cape Carson Gazette.

Reporter Bitten by Snake!

I wanted to *write* the news, not *be* it!

Counting the apartment numbers, we continued along to number six. The bathroom window was partly open. Standing on tippy-toe, I peered inside to see an empty bathroom and a glimpse of the darkened unit beyond.

'Give me a leg up,' I told Kim.

'Are you sure about this?' Kim asked. 'Technically, you're breaking and entering.'

'What are you now? A lawyer? Hoist me up.'

Groaning, Kim gave me a leg-up and I hauled myself through the slim gap. There was a terrible moment when I got stuck, and another even more horrifying headline flashed through my mind:

Local Journalist Caught in Foiled Bathroom Heist

Driving it from my mind, I grabbed a shower railing and somehow clambered into the room without breaking my neck. Holding my breath, I listened for movement.

'Rosie?' Kim hissed. 'What are you doing?'

'I'm wrestling a crocodile!' I snapped. 'What do you think I'm doing? Be quiet for a moment. I'm looking around.'

There were a few cosmetics on the bench. A beige lipstick that would never have suited me. Some moisturising lotion. A hairbrush.

That fits with it being a woman.

At least there wasn't the horrible smell of a decomposing body. Come to think of it, I'd never smelt a decomposing body, but I imagined I'd know it when I encountered one. I crept into the next room. One wall was red brick, probably fashionable fifty years ago, but now it just looked cheap and ugly.

There was also grey stucco on the ceiling with a saucer-shaped light fitting in the middle. A built-in wardrobe occupied one corner. A tiny chest of drawers huddled in another. The only other item of furniture was the double bed, and even this had a lean.

This place really is a dive.

A suitcase sat on the bed.

What's in there?

Before I could investigate further, I heard an engine—and froze. A white sedan ground to a halt beyond the closed curtain. I watched in horror as a shadowy figure—a man—emerged from the vehicle.

He's coming here.

Call it a sixth sense. Call it paranoia. Either way, I was sure he was about to enter the unit. Heart thudding, I looked around wildly for somewhere to hide. Taking refuge in the bathroom would work for all of five seconds. There was no way I could scramble out the window in time. The wardrobe was too small and a great place to get hacked to death by a murderer.

The only place to hide was the most obvious place of all.

I dove under the bed just as a key was pushed into the lock. There was a rattle, and then the door opened.

The noise of the outside world blared briefly as the man entered. Then the door shut, and the room was deathly quiet again. I didn't move a muscle, breathing shallowly through my mouth as I listened for the occupant.

He was still. It was as if he were listening too. *Does he know I'm here? Is he about to drag me out from hiding?* His feet moved on the carpet—and then he strode into the bathroom. Whoever had turned up was in a hurry. He left the bathroom, and I heard the suitcase *clack* open. There was the moving about of belongings.

What's going on?

I glimpsed boots moving about the room. The foot size was big. I held my breath as the figure lingered beside the bed. If he looked under here, I was a goner. How would I ever explain this?

I'm with room service. Oh yes. We always clean under the beds like this. How else would you pick up that pesky chewing gum?

No. That would not work. The man moved again, this time heading back to the suitcase. The bag snapped shut. Then the figure crossed to the door, left and deathly silence filled the room once more.

An engine roared to life outside.

Time to move.

Scrambling from under the bed, I raced to the window just in time to see Kim emerging from behind a bush.

'Are you all right?' she hissed. 'I didn't dare say anything in case—'

'He's getting away! Help me out!'

'Who's getting away?' Kim asked as she dragged me out the window.

'I didn't see his face, but he just emptied the room and is driving off.'

'Is he the killer?'

'He's not her manicurist,' I said as we rounded the building to see a white sedan pull into the street.

We sprinted to my jeep and piled in with Trixie barking with excitement. She could always tell when things were afoot.

'Follow that car!' Kim yelled, adding, 'I always wanted to say that.'

We flew down the back streets of Cape Carson. The vehicle was some distance ahead, and I accelerated, tearing around corners as it disappeared around bends. Reaching Percy Street, the car turned left and out of sight.

We can't let it get away!

I reached Percy Street just as a slow-moving truck appeared on my right. Pulling out, I cut it off, and the truck driver angrily blared his horn.

'He doesn't sound happy,' Kim said.

'Too bad!'

We were soon on the winding road heading east out of town. The Great Coastal Road angled upwards with steep hills on our left and a sharp drop to the ocean on our right. Beyond the drop lay rocks below and the vast expanse of the Southern

Ocean. The whole journey along this section of the coast was like this: sharp bends with a guard rail on the other side. More than once, though, cars had crashed through and landed on the rocky shoreline.

I glimpsed the other vehicle disappearing around the next turn.

'I think he knows we're following him,' I said.

Trixie barked in agreement.

'What are you going to do?' Kim asked.

'The only thing I can do. Go faster.'

I sped around the winding corners. Kim let out a gasp as we came around one corner on the wrong side of the road and spotted an oncoming car. It blared its horn, and I dragged us back to the right side. Even Trixie gave a worried whine.

Reaching a straighter section of road, I poured on the speed, then braked hard as we reached the corner. I was just in time to see the other car disappearing again—but at least now we were closer! Speeding up again, I reached another slight curve in the road, a section that swung inland. I touched the brake, but then spied a dark patch on the road at the same moment.

Oil!

I braked again, but I'd already hit the patch.

The car slid.

And spun.

I saw the guard railing facing the ocean, beyond which lay

the deadly drop to the rocks below. Then there was a flash of the cliff face. I desperately turned the steering wheel to keep us on the road, but it was to no avail as the car pitched sideways towards the hill.

16

A familiar face appeared over the side of the embankment. 'You ladies okay?' Todd Parker asked. 'I came around the bend just in time to see you practicing your stunt driving. Good thing you didn't go through the fence on the other side, though. It's quite a drop.'

I thought of how far a drop—and swallowed.

'We're fine,' I said, a trifle defensively. 'Just a little shaken.'

We lay at a forty-five-degree angle in the roadside ditch. One side lay against the embankment; the other side was in the air. I wasn't hurt—but I was embarrassed. The last person I'd expected to see was Todd Parker. At least it wasn't the killer. Or was it? It seemed very odd that Todd had turned up just as we'd lost our murder suspect. Surely...

No. Todd Parker couldn't be the person we were pursuing. Could he?

'You'll need a tow truck to right the vehicle,' he said.

With Todd and Kim's help, we could push my jeep into an

upright position, but not without possibly causing an injury to one of us. I didn't want to risk that.

'Sure,' I said.

'I can order one,' Todd offered. 'Can you climb out?'

I told him we could. Kim got out first, taking Trixie with her. Finally, I scrambled up the short incline, Todd gripping my hand to haul me to safety.

'I'm a good driver,' I said before realising how silly that sounded under the circumstances. 'I hit oil.'

'I can see that.' His tone was gentle. 'I've already radioed the fire department to be safe. They'll be here shortly.'

He headed off, leaving me to peer in dismay at my car. I groaned. My car already had a thousand dents and scratches. I didn't need any more.

Kim sidled over. 'You're not going to tell your cop friend about the killer?'

'And admit to breaking into that hotel? Not likely.' Todd Parker was back in his vehicle making a call. 'Look.'

'What?'

'Look at his car,' I hissed. 'He's driving a white sedan!'

'But it's a Holden,' she said. 'Wasn't the other one a Hyundai?'

I wasn't sure. My mind ticked over. Could Todd Parker be the killer?

No, I thought. *That's ridiculous.*

Still…

It took half an hour for a tow truck to arrive. It reversed up in front of my car. The driver climbed out, expertly put the car into neutral, and attached a towline. Minutes later, the jeep was upright on the road. It looked like the scrapes weren't as bad as I'd first thought. More dirt than damage.

'Do you mind if we have a word?' Todd asked, eyeing Kim and motioning me behind my vehicle. I wondered if he were about to chastise me for my driving or warn me off following him around. 'I'm kind of new to town.'

'Uh, yes.'

What's this about?

'How about dinner one night?' he asked.

'Huh?'

'You know dinner? People sit around a table. Eat food. Share conversation.'

Wow. Dinner with a potential killer. Something else stirred in my chest. Dinner with a nice-looking guy. *Hmm.* I wasn't sure if I should feel flattered or worried.

But what was that saying? Keep your friends close, but your enemies even closer? Suppose Todd Parker murdered the woman at the Bailey house. He might let something slip in conversation. And if he were innocent, we'd just have a lovely evening together.

'I might be available,' I said. 'What kind of food?'

'I'm trying to eat food that isn't a protein bar. How about pizza?'

'I can go with that.'

'I'll let you be my guide.'

'Giovanni's does the best pizza in town.'

We coordinated calendars and made a date. Kim tactfully sauntered over after Todd wished me well and drove off.

'What do you think?' I asked as he disappeared around the bend.

'Amazing. Especially those biceps—'

'No! I mean, was that the car we were chasing?'

'You really think he's the killer?' Kim frowned. 'I doubt it. The other car was more run down. And the number plate was smeared with dirt.'

I felt a little better now. She'd had a better chance of studying the car than me. Climbing back into my jeep, we headed back to town where I dropped Kim off at her place. I continued on to Sandy's Diner to grab a coffee.

'Did Harry tell you about the festival?' Sandy asked as I settled onto a bar stool.

'Huh?'

'I rang the office and spoke to Harry about the rock and roll festival!'

Now that I thought about it, Harry had mentioned that people were trying to arrange another festival for the town.

There'd been talk about it, but so far, it had remained just that: talk. The town already had several festivals. It thrived on holding events that attracted people from all around the district.

'We're having a committee meeting tomorrow after work,' Sandy said as she handed me my coffee. 'Be nice if you could be there.'

I grumbled silently to myself. *A reporter's job is never done.* Checking my diary, I found an empty spot. 'I'll be there,' I promised, taking a sip of my jumbo double-shot caramel latte. My brain and body immediately felt better. 'Oh boy. That hits the spot.'

Thanking her, I then headed to the office where I found Harry at his desk.

'What?' he said. 'You still work here?'

'I try to squeeze in a few hours when I can.'

He asked me how my inquiries into the Baileys' deaths had progressed, and I told him I'd spoken to Lily and John. Harry immediately seized on the ghost story angle. He liked the idea of splashing it all over the front page.

'Do we have to do that?' I groaned. 'Maybe we can be a little less sensational and stick to the facts.'

'Can you at least do a sidebar? People love ghost stories. Even people who don't believe in ghosts love them. Gives them something to argue about.'

'How about you? Do you believe in ghosts?'

'My mother swore till the day she died that she grew up in a haunted house. I didn't believe her. Still, the older you get, the more you wonder about that stuff. Maybe the divide between this world and the next isn't as solid as we think.'

Nodding thoughtfully, I headed through to my office to find a pile of messages waiting for me. I glanced over at Jay.

'Your phone's been ringing off the hook,' he said. 'You're a popular woman.'

I groaned. 'Great.'

He glanced back at the article he was working on. 'I'm not sure about this word,' he said. 'Is it slither or sliver when you're talking about a snake?'

'It's the one you find in the dictionary,' I said, picking up the first of the messages. 'Now, let me look through these.'

'…should be the biggest event the town's ever seen,' Sandy said. 'We just need to work together to make it happen.'

It had been a good meeting and far better attended than I'd expected. We'd met at Sandy's place, which she shared with her partner, Tilly. Whereas Sandy looked like she could wrestle a crocodile, Tilly was dainty, like a young Winona Ryder.

It always surprised me that Tilly shared Sandy's love of motorcycles. More than once, I'd watched them roar past me on their Harley-Davidson Cruisers along the Great Coastal Road.

Sandy's house didn't look too different from the diner. Rock and roll paraphernalia covered the walls, and there was even a pinball machine and a jukebox in the corner. Everyone grouped around for a picture. I took several as you never knew when someone would be blinking or winking.

'Looks like this might be a happening thing,' I said. 'It can join our long list of festivals: the Cupcake festival, the Zombie march, Book week—'

'—and the Sci-fi weekend,' Sandy said. 'Well, you can never have too many festivals.'

On the way back to my car, I felt a drop of water on my cheek. The sky had turned dark during the meeting. There was a single rolling rumble of thunder and rain began to tumble down. I ran for my car. *Might be a good night for lasagne and a huddle in front of the television.* Just as I started the engine, my phone rang. I groaned when I saw the caller.

Not now.

'They're back!' Edna yelled before I could utter a word.

'What?'

'The killer! Or the ghost!' She paused. 'Or the killer ghost! I'm not sure. I saw them in the attic window!'

I hung up, promising that I'd come over straight away. Going to the Bailey house alone to face whatever lurked there—whether it be a ghost, a person, or something else—was pushing my luck. *I need backup.* Quickly ringing Kim, I was relieved when she agreed to accompany me.

By the time I reached the Bailey place, the rain was coming down hard. A sharp onshore breeze was pushing it inland, whipping the giant eucalypts around town into a frenzy.

Kim's white Ford Focus trundled into the street and drew to a halt. Taking advantage of the rain momentarily subsiding to a drizzle, I wrapped my arms around myself and raced over.

Trixie barked excitedly at my side.

'Look at this weather!' I yelled.

'Isn't it great?'

I'd forgotten Kim loved storms. One time I'd caught her walking down the beach under a metal framed umbrella while a thunderstorm was in full swing. Visiting a haunted house in a downpour was probably as much fun as watching *Night of the Living Dead* for the hundredth time.

'Come on,' I said. 'Let's go inside.'

We made our way to the front door and opened it as a crack of thunder rumbled across the sky. It wouldn't be dark for hours, but the storm had brought night early. I activated the light on my mobile phone and cast it around the gloomy interior. Nothing had changed from our previous visits.

At least, that's what I thought.

'Look!' I said.

The painting in the hallway of the Bailey family members had seemed to stare down at us the last time we entered the room. My blood ran cold as I stared at it now. It was still on the wall—*but now it was upside down.*

Trixie gave a low whine.

'Wow,' Kim breathed. 'There must be a poltergeist here.'

'Or a prankster,' I said, swallowing. 'Edna said she saw someone up in the attic. We should be careful.'

Bang! Bang! Bang!

I turned to Kim. 'Were they...gunshots?'

'Probably just a loose board somewhere.' Kim stopped to consider. 'Or it's Justin and Claire Bailey, now a shadowy pair of disembodied spirits doomed to relive the last horrible moments of their lives for all eternity.'

'Yeah,' I said. 'Or that.'

We started up the stairs but had only taken a few steps when Kim grabbed my arm.

'What's that sound?' she asked.

I listened hard. There was the sound of the wind. A distant roll of thunder. The whoosh of trees churning in the wind. The creaking timbers of the house. And—

Music.

'What is it?'

'It's a classical piece,' I said. 'Something by Beethoven.'

Kim was breathless. 'I know what it is,' she said. '*Für Elise.*'

'The record on the gramophone?'

The music grew louder as we climbed the stairs. I suggested to Kim that the storm may have caused a power surge that brought the player to life. She didn't reply, and even I thought it was a poor explanation. We mounted the final stairs to the attic, my phone shaking badly in my hand. I aimed it over the empty room. Nothing. The music continued to play as we breathlessly crossed to the gramophone. I stared in horror as the record spun hypnotically on the turntable. After lifting off the needle, silence filled the room until it was broken by a distant roll of thunder.

'We'd better search the rest of the house,' I said.

Bang! Bang! Bang!

I almost dropped my phone.

'It's that same sound again,' Kim said. 'It could be a ghost—or worse.'

I wasn't sure what *worse* could be. We had to methodically search every room of the house. We began by rechecking the secret staircase. After finding the door at the bottom was still latched, we almost ran back up the stairs to the attic. Then we made our way down the main stairs and went through each room on the first floor before returning to ground. Entering the living room, the shadows danced as my light moved across the chamber.

Kim gasped. 'Look!' she said, pointing.

My gaze followed her outstretched hand. I swallowed. *The painting was back around the right way!* 'Someone's playing games with us,' I said hoarsely. 'There's someone else in the house.'

'We've already searched upstairs!'

'Then we need to search the rest of this floor and the basement too,' I said. 'And have your keys ready.'

'But they won't fit any locks,' Kim said.

'No! To use as a weapon! Remember, aim for the eyes!'

We got out our keys, ready to apply an old-fashioned eye gouge to any evildoers intent on causing us harm.

Trixie barked as we made our way down the stairs to the basement. The storm still raged outside. Lightning flickered through the casement window as my eyes took in the gloomy corners. Generations of spiders had made their homes down here, and dust had accumulated for decades. I could almost hear Nan's voice in my head. *This place needs a good clean.* Well, she was right.

Bang! Bang! Bang!

This time it came from above, but no one could have evaded us; we'd searched every room on the way down. There was no way anyone could be in the house.

Kim's voice shook. 'What's causing that sound?'

'Come on,' I said, almost dragging her back up the stairs.

We returned to the living room and—

The painting was upside down again!

And that's when the screaming began. It wasn't Kim or me. It was a prolonged shriek of utter terror that rang out from the attic high above us. The woman's scream was followed by *no no no* and then a man's voice raised in anger. A voice so furious it was more like an animalistic snarl than a person. Then there were more screams, a final shriek, and then—

18

'And then what happened?' Ellie asked.

She and I were huddled around Doris's desk at the Cape Carson Gazette. It was early the following morning, and I was already armed with my first coffee for the day.

'And then we ran,' I said. 'I'm not even sure how I got outside. All I know is that one minute we were in the living room, the next I was outside in the storm with Kim.'

'And then?' Doris asked.

That's where Kim and I parted ways. I watched as she drove off. Or tried to, anyway. She'd first mounted the curb before sideswiping someone's garbage bins and cutting a corner. I'd sat in silence in my own vehicle, shaking as I tried to process it all. None of it made sense.

It was beyond the realm of believability.

And yet, it had happened.

'I can't explain it,' I said, thinking. 'There's got to be a rational explanation, but I don't know what it is.'

The office's front door flew open and Harry Blackshore stumbled in. Although the rain had subsided, a westerly wind was blowing hard. The editor muttered something about it being great weather for ducks before stomping into his office.

Following him in, I related what had happened as he put his things down and settled behind his desk.

'I don't suppose you got any good pictures?' he asked.

'Um, no.'

'Amazing,' he said. 'Everyone carries a camera, but nobody thinks to snap pictures of ghosts and aliens when they appear.'

'I was too busy being terrified.'

He thrummed his fingers on the desk. 'Well,' he said. 'I've got the front page planned, but there's still a gap.'

Bringing up his computer, Harry showed me the pictures that he'd chosen for my story. One was a picture I'd taken outside the house. The others were older. Some interior shots and then another which appeared to have come from a lifestyle spread.

It was really something to behold. The photo had been taken in the attic. Claire rested on the vintage chaise lounge. Justin stood at the bar. The bird, Spencer, hung in his cage. The room was jammed with furniture, decorations and the Bose sound system.

The cabinets were filled with mementos from the theatre. Jamming the corners were theatre mannequins: a medieval fool, a life-size ballerina, a bear.

Judging by the date on the picture, it had been taken a week before their deaths. I shivered. It was strange to think that Justin and Claire would be dead a week later. They didn't look gloriously happy in the picture. Neither did they look unhappy. There was nothing in their faces to show what was brewing beneath the surface.

'A ghost story would be the icing on the cake,' Harry said, his eyes angling up to me.

'Lily and John won't be happy about that.'

'Ghost stories sell—and I can deal with Lily and John.'

Harry was always telling me that he'd deal with complaints, but nine times out of ten, it was me facing the unhappy public. Regardless, I said I'd put something together.

The rest of the morning passed with me writing a sidebar about what had happened on my most recent visit to the Bailey house. Leaving Kim out of the story, I wrote about the painting, the gramophone, and the sounds of gunshots and screams. Once I'd finished writing, I read through it again. It all sounded so outrageous that even I doubted it was true—and I'd lived through it!

The next thing I did was put a short piece together about the proposed rock and roll festival. There wasn't a lot of detail yet. That would come closer to the date. At least I had a good picture of the organising committee.

Like Harry always said, the our paper was about three things and one thing all at once: pictures, pictures, pictures.

Today was publishing day and the tension in the office grew more palpable as the afternoon rolled on. It was always like this just before we put the paper to bed. After making the final changes, we sent the files to Coles Printery up the road. They worked till midnight to produce it, and then a transportation service hand-delivered the finished product to people's letter-boxes the following morning.

It was after five by the time I finally left work. The sky had cleared during the afternoon and was now peacock blue, smeared with white and charcoal cloud. Lingering on the main street with Trixie at my side, we stared up at the sight.

The most beautiful thing I've seen all day, I thought. *And it's free.*

Trixie gave a happy bark, and I patted her head.

'A quiet night in front of the TV might be best for us,' I said. 'Maybe even some leftovers.'

My phone beeped.

What's that...?

I peered down at the screen—and yelled.

Trixie barked as we climbed into my jeep. 'I've got a date,' I said, jamming my foot on the accelerator. 'And I'd forgotten all about it.' Minutes later, I arrived back home, where I found Dave's car parked in the driveway. Inside, Dave and Nan were busy in the kitchen.

'You look flushed,' Nan said, a cheeky glimmer in her eye. 'What have you been up to—and with whom?'

'It's nothing like that!' I retorted. 'I'm late!'

'For a date?' she said. 'Oh, I remember now. You're seeing that hunky new policeman. What's his name?'

'Todd Parker.'

Nan continued to speak, but I was peering past her at Dave, who was busy stirring something in a pot on the stove.

Wow. That smells good.

'Were you a chef?' I asked him.

'A locksmith,' he said. 'But I've got a few dishes that are my specialty. Tried and true recipes that even I can't stuff up.'

I tried to imagine Dave as a locksmith. It was far easier to imagine him cracking safes than fixing locks.

Still, he seemed oddly domesticated as he shuffled around the kitchen, stirring the contents of pots. I hurried to my bedroom, tried on six outfits and three pairs of shoes, finally settling on a green dress I hadn't worn for a long time.

Applying makeup on the run, I tripped over my own feet just as I reached the living room and went sprawling.

I jumped up again. 'I'm fine!'

By now, Trixie was in as much of a state as me. Calming her down, I wished her goodnight before racing to the car. Soon, I was in the front lobby of Giovanni's, my eyes searching the muted pale-yellow light. The place was almost empty. Maybe Todd hadn't—

I swallowed. Todd was waiting near the bar, his eyes on me. He wore a pair of what appeared to be new jeans, a checkered black-and-white shirt, and a jacket. He smiled as I approached, but then I spotted a furrow in his brow as I drew near.

Why is he staring at me like that?

'Hey,' he said. 'I was worried you'd stood me up.'

'I was being fashionably late.'

We settled at a table near the window and ordered drinks. This position gave us a fantastic view of the water. Night was falling, and the ocean was a shimmering plain of azure blue. The high cloud was crimson from the last light of day. It was a beautiful sight.

'It's a lovely night,' I commented.

'Very nice,' he said. 'That's a pretty outfit you're wearing.'

'Thanks.' I felt flattered, but then I had to remind myself of the previous day's accident. *He might be a killer.* My eyes met his, and my fear turned to confusion. *He's staring again. Is it my dress?* I glanced down at my outfit. 'This was just an old thing I threw on.'

'It's an interesting style.'

'Oh?' I wasn't sure why he was so interested in my dress, so I changed subjects. I told him about my career, how I ended up in Cape Carson, and my marriage breaking up. 'And how are you finding the town?'

He shrugged. 'It's fine,' he said. 'Different to Melbourne.'

'Cape Carson's different to everywhere.' I looked past him. 'Oh, dear.'

Todd's glance followed mine. 'What is it?'

George entered with Blossom close behind.

I groaned. *What is this? Are George and Blossom stalking me?* I quickly explained who they were to Todd.

'I see,' Todd said. 'You're not about to get into a brawl, are you? I'd hate to arrest you. Especially on a first date.'

'Let's leave the handcuffs for the second date,' I said, then realised how that sounded. 'I mean...no handcuffs...I mean...'

'Oh hello,' George said as he neared our table. 'We keep running into you everywhere.'

'I get around,' I said, watching George's eyes angle to Todd. 'This is Todd. A friend.'

George and Todd shook hands, and I was suddenly struck by how similar they looked. I frowned. *Is that why I agreed to go out with Todd? Because he reminds me of George?* No, that was silly. Interestingly, Blossom seemed to be taking more interest in Todd than George. Her eyes opened a little wider as she played with a strand of her hair.

George's eyes narrowed. 'Hang on,' he said. '*Todd Parker*? I recognize you now. You were the star of that kid's show. What was it?'

Todd gave an almost imperceptible roll of his eyes. 'The Rusty Jones Mysteries,' he said.

I stared at him. No wonder he seemed familiar when I first met him! The TV series had been on when I was a kid. Rusty Jones and his band of intrepid friends investigated mysteries in a seaside town called Kalua Bay.

'A movie star,' Blossom said, sighing. 'Goodness.'

She looked ready to swoon.

'That was all a long time ago,' Todd said.

'And so you're a cop now,' George said.

'Now I do the real thing.'

George glanced over at Blossom and noticed her starry-eyed expression. His brow creased. He said they'd better grab their table and headed off. I took a sip of water as I stared into Todd's face. It was obvious now that it was pointed out. No wonder I thought him familiar. At one time, The Rusty Jones Mysteries had been one of the biggest shows on television. Todd had played Rusty, the leader of the group. His companions had been a girl named Louise and a stocky little kid called Preston.

'Wow,' I said. 'I didn't know I'd come out with a celebrity.'

This time Todd rolled his eyes for real. 'That was all a long time ago,' he said. 'It was painful, to be honest. The other kids at school gave me a hard time about being an actor. By the time the series wrapped, I'd fallen well behind in my studies. I thought I'd always be acting, but it didn't work out that way.

I was so well known from the series it was hard to do anything else.'

'So you ended up becoming a cop?'

'It was either that or a bodybuilder.'

'That was in the cards?'

'My Dad would have preferred that.' There was something about the way he said it that didn't invite comment. 'He was the driver of my career.'

We sat in silence for a moment, and I stared out at the darkness.

Todd finally spoke up. 'The investigation side was probably the one good thing to come out of the series,' he said. 'The mysteries in the show were contrived, but the solutions always made sense.'

'And you worked as part of a *team*,' I said pointedly.

Todd raised an eyebrow. 'I *work* with a team at the station,' he said. 'A team of experienced cops. People who carry guns and get fingerprints and work off a nationwide database.'

'There's a lot to be said for amateur detectives.'

He laughed. 'You're Sherlock Holmes now?'

I remembered Kim comparing us to Holmes and Watson. 'Not at all.'

Todd shook his head. 'And I can't have a member of the public—especially a reporter—helping me investigate crime.'

'Sure you can,' I said. 'But we've got to be honest with each other.'

He frowned. 'And you mean…'

'How's your health?'

'Health?'

'Specifically, your eye health.' I waited to see if he would say something, but he just pursed his lips. 'You remember I pointed out that sailing ship to you at Cut Rock? Except it wasn't a sailing ship. It was a freighter. Even someone who knows nothing about ships can tell the difference. The only person who couldn't—'

'Would be someone with eye problems.' Todd let out a long breath. 'They're cataracts. Early-onset. Rare for someone to get them at my age, but it's not unheard of.'

'So when are you getting them operated on?'

'I'll get them done. Eventually.'

'And it's not affecting your work?'

He reddened, and I realised it was the wrong thing to say.

'Sorry,' I hastened. 'I didn't mean to interfere.'

'I'm not one for doctors,' Todd said, not looking up. 'The last one I went to was years ago.'

'Really?'

'My dad always said that real men didn't go to doctors.'

'That sounds kind of dumb.'

This time, Todd's mouth set into a hard line, and I realised I had pushed things too far. Fortunately, our food arrived at that moment, and I quickly changed the topic. I told him it was difficult meeting people when I first moved to Cape Carson, so I'd made a point of getting involved with a local group.

'What was it?' he asked.

'The Cape Carson Mystery Book Club,' I said, explaining that we read a different mystery novel every month. 'That's how I met Kim. We became friends straight away.'

'Have you ever done any writing yourself? Creative writing, I mean.'

I blushed. 'Well...'

Todd laughed. 'Tell me!' he said. 'Confess!'

Groaning, I told him that I'd written some short stories and was currently working on my first novel. I rarely spoke about my writing attempts. The short stories had been challenging, but making the book work was proving a near impossibility.

Still, Todd appeared interested. 'That's great,' he said. 'What's your subject? Romance? Adventure? Sci-fi...'

'Uh, mystery stories.'

His eyes twinkled. 'Why am I not surprised?'

'It's just something I do in my spare time. I haven't even tried to get anything published.'

'And any other hobbies?'

I told him Kim and I shared movie nights, and we used to visit the Palladium together.

'The old cinema on Percy Street?'

'It's closed now. Back then, the Palladium was showing all the old Hitchcock films. Even the silent ones.'

'What's your favourite Hitchcock?'

That was a tough question. 'So many of them are good,' I said. 'A lot of people love Vertigo, but I think mine is Dial M for Murder. Ray Milland is *so* good at being bad!'

'And Grace Kelly is always fantastic.'

'You know your films!'

Todd laughed. 'I like old mystery movies!'

'So,' I said. 'That's something else we've got in common.'

19

'Okay,' Kim said. 'Tell me everything!'

We were sitting in her office at the Cape Carson Public Library, where she worked as the head librarian. The building was a sprawling modern place with a curving front of glass and timber panels. Kim's office was located behind the main borrowing desk and adjacent to the new release shelves.

'There's not much to tell,' I said.

She deadpanned. 'Rosie Ryan,' she said. 'That's possibly the silliest thing you've ever said. Now—spill!'

Sighing, I told her that dinner had been pleasant, although Todd seemed a little reserved. He hadn't kissed me goodnight at my car, but I was okay with that. I wasn't the kind to take things too fast.

'Nice,' Kim said, nodding with approval. 'So he's a gentleman.'

'Very much so.' I paused. 'There was one problem.'

'What was it?'

'I was wearing my dress backwards.'

'Huh?'

'Relax.' She looked so amazed that embarrassment turned my face red. 'I don't think he noticed.'

'Are you sure?'

'Yes! Totally!' I said, although I wasn't. 'Now enough about my love life. Why did you ask me to drop in?'

Kim sighed and shook her head. 'Okay,' she said. 'You'll be pleased to hear that I've been doing some research.'

I sat up. In addition to being head librarian, and local history expert, Kim had a Masters in Information Management; her research skills were *par excellence*. 'What have you found out?' I asked.

'Quite a bit,' Kim said, opening a manilla folder. 'I looked up The Grange. You recall that was the theatre Justin Bailey owned in Melbourne? It turns out the place was a mess when he bought it. A *real* mess. There was even talk about knocking it down because it was in such poor shape. I discovered that Justin had to borrow from all over the place to pay for its restoration. Some of the money came from less than reputable sources.'

'What do you mean?'

'News reports mentioned organised crime. Someone who lent Justin money was shot dead in a gangland shooting a few weeks after The Grange was sold.'

I thought about this. Could Justin and Claire's deaths be gang-related? Melbourne had a long history of rival crime gangs. It's possible that Justin annoyed the wrong person, and they decided to take retribution. Maybe it was even the reason why they left Melbourne and came to Cape Carson.

Except...

The manner of their deaths didn't fit with being gangland hits. Those murders usually took place in the back alleys of Melbourne or after a knock at a suburban front door. Not hundreds of kilometres from Melbourne in a quiet seaside town. And there'd been no mention of unusual visitors to the house. The names of prominent crime figures would have come up in the police investigation, even if Justin and Claire's deaths were considered a murder-suicide.

'Could Justin have owed the wrong people money?' I asked. 'Was he in debt?'

'I don't think so.' Kim peered down at her notes. 'I had to hobble together some figures and make a few guestimates, but it looks like he probably walked away with two million in profit.'

'And that's after all his bills were paid?'

Kim nodded. 'Two million dollars is a lot of money,' she said, 'but it was worth even more back then. After building his house, he probably still had a bundle.'

'Any idea what he did with the excess?'

She picked up another page. 'That brings me to my next piece of research: the property in Northville.'

'Where the winery is?'

'It wasn't a winery back then. Just a hundred acres of land. I couldn't find the exact details, but it looks like John and Lily shared equally in both the Cape Carson house and the Northville land. Although, you know there's a caveat regarding the house?'

'I know.' I told Kim what Lily had said. 'That place is going to be part of Cape Carson for the better part of the next century—whether we like it or not.'

'And that can't make life any easier for either John or Lily. The house isn't leased or earning an income. With council rates, it must cost a fortune to own.' Kim referred to her notes again. 'From what I've been able to work out, I think there was also some money in an account that John and Lily received after their parents' deaths. I believe Lily bought out John's share and started the winery.'

I thought back to my conversation with Lily. From what she'd said, it sounded like everything had been sunk into the business. I mentioned this to Kim.

'That's not surprising,' she said. 'Wineries don't make money right away. You probably won't make anything for at least five years, and that's being optimistic. It could take ten or longer before you start making a profit.'

'Sheesh,' I said. 'Remind me not to start a winery.'

'You'd be better off taking up share trading.'

'Like John Bailey?'

'Absolutely. I don't know how much money he's made over the years, but I'm sure it's a lot. There's a private company connected to his name that owns three properties. I suspect he's doing very well for himself.'

I rubbed my chin. 'So John and Lily both profited from their parents' deaths. Of course, they were both still young at the time. Lily was fifteen, and John was sixteen. They were surely too young to have committed the murders.'

'Children have killed their parents before,' Kim pointed out.

'True. But Lily was in her bedroom, and John was in the kitchen with Wayne and Sofia when their parents died. It meant Lily had to get to the attic, kill her parents, and return to her room again before other people were on the scene.' I shook my head. 'That didn't happen. She emerged at the bottom of the attic stairs at the same time as everyone else. Plus, the attic door was locked from the inside. Wayne Price had to break it in.'

Kim sighed. 'This is always much easier for Holmes and Watson,' she said. 'The simplest explanation is that Baileys' deaths were a murder-suicide.'

'Except some people heard two gunshots, and others heard

three.'

Hattie, one of the other librarians, appeared at the door and told Kim they had a problem with the room booking system. Kim groaned. 'That's been playing up all week,' she said, turning to me. 'One of the rooms got double-booked to both The Knitting Circle and the Pressed Flowers Society.' She shook her head. 'Those old ladies can be *really* feisty.'

We made our way to the door.

'One thing,' Kim added. 'You should chat to Mina.'

'Mina?'

'She's doing cataloguing at the moment. I found out that Mina went to school with Lily and John.'

I shook my head in admiration. 'Kim Chen,' I said. 'You're incredible.'

'I know. Let's keep it quiet though. I like people to think I'm merely mortal.'

She directed me to a room at the back where I found Mina, a Persian woman with soft, dark eyes, sitting at her computer. These eyes were staring at the screen in confusion.

'Do you have a minute?' I asked.

Mina looked up. 'Absolutely!' she said, pushing back from her computer. 'Anything to escape MARC.'

'MARC?'

'Bibliographic fields in library records.' She held up an old pamphlet. 'I'm trying to catalogue this. *Aaarrggg!*'

Laughing, I sat down and told her I was trying to learn more about John and Lily Bailey. Mina nodded thoughtfully. 'Those two,' she said. 'Well, not just them. That whole family was completely dysfunctional.'

'In what way?'

'Okay,' she said. 'John and Lily were rich—and they didn't try to hide it either. The other kids resented them for that.'

'I see.'

'And they were full of themselves. Especially John'

'In what way?'

'Well, he would boast about how much they had. And John had a real—what would you call it—swagger. It's like he knew he came from a rich family and everything would always be fine.' Mina sighed. 'Except, it wasn't. That was an awful year for him, even apart from his parents' deaths.'

'How do you mean?'

'I don't remember it too well. He was dating a girl—what was her name?' Mina frowned in concentration. 'Erin. That's it. Erin Fowler. She was really nice. I don't know what she saw in John, but she seemed to see through his bravado and money, and seemed to like him.'

'What happened?'

'She died about a week before John's parents.'

'What?' This was news to me. 'I didn't know that.'

'Erin had a severe peanut allergy. One day at school, her

sandwich accidentally got swapped with one of her friends. Of all things, it was peanut butter. It turns out she didn't have her medication with her, and she died.'

That's terrible, I thought. *No wonder John wants to forget the past.*

'And you knew Lily?' I said.

Mina nodded. 'Lily was in my year at school—and she was awful. A monster. She'd be fine one minute and awful the next. Lily would fly into a temper if someone said the wrong thing or took something of hers without asking.'

'Really?' I found this hard to equate with the woman I'd met. 'Was she violent?'

'Yes. A few times. She broke someone's nose once.'

Mina didn't remember much more about the Bailey kids, saying it was all a long time ago. Thanking her, I headed back into the library. It was busy now. A school group had arrived, and a line was forming at the checkout desk. The kids were laughing and shoving each other. It reminded me of my own days at school. They were a mixture of pleasure and pain. Mostly, I had a good time but I also got teased a lot because of my height.

Making my way out, I crossed to the post where I'd left Trixie. She sat up and gave me a reproachful look. 'Don't be like that,' I said. 'I'm trying to track down a killer.'

Although, I thought. *I'm no closer than I was before.*

20

Harry leaned around the doorway into my office. 'A woman's body has been found on Kelsie Beach,' he said.

I glanced up from my computer. It had been a big day. Actually, a big night and day. I'd gone to bed at a decent hour, taken Trixie for an early morning walk, and arrived at work to face a deluge of phone calls about the Bailey house. Harry's editorial instinct had been correct. Everyone was ringing up with their own ghost stories about the place. A follow-up story was definitely in the cards. Now, though, it looked like that had to be on the backburner.

'A drowning?' I asked.

There's a saying in journalism: *if it bleeds, it leads.*

'Probably,' Harry said. 'Although no one's been reported missing.'

Kelsie Beach was only about ten kilometres down the coast. 'I'll take a drive down and see what I can find,' I said.

Minutes later, I was heading down the coast with Trixie at

my side.

The weather bureau had predicted scattered showers, and it was right. Banks of cloud tumbled across the sky, dropping brief showers every few minutes.

The Great Coastal Road has dozens of places where you can turn off to take a break. Some are lookouts perched on the ocean side of the road. Others are inlets where you can park and wander about a secluded beach. Kelsie Beach is one of them. It's a peaceful place to stop and admire the view, but a dangerous place to go for a dip. The currents can be treacherous, and swimmers can quickly get into trouble.

A police vehicle and ambulance had stopped at the beach. It looked like a few passers-by had pulled over to see what was happening too. Parking beside them, I scrambled down the stairs and found Todd and Jim Turner at the scene.

Constable Turner had formed a human barrier between himself and the few people on the shoreline. Under a sheet on the beach lay a shape I assumed was the body. A sudden breeze came up, and the sheet flipped over. I glimpsed a woman, Asian in appearance and wearing slacks and a jumper. Todd quickly covered her up again.

'Everyone back,' Jim said, although it didn't look like people were taking any notice. I suspected that Jim just liked to throw his weight around.

All right, I thought. *Let's go with Plan B.*

'Constable Turner,' I said. 'Have you been able to identify the body?'

'Not yet. It's still early days.'

'What can you tell me?'

'Only that we've identified a woman of Asian appearance. Aged between forty and fifty. Possibly a visitor to the area. Appears to have drowned—'

'So she fell off a boat?'

Jim Turner stared at me. 'What makes you think that?'

'Not many people go swimming fully clothed.' I nodded to the ocean. 'And it hasn't been beach weather lately.'

The geeky constable was flustered. 'Our investigation is on-going,' he said, using the oldest cop line in the book. 'We'll put out a press statement when we know more.'

'How's the board game going?' I asked.

Jim brightened up. 'A Steam car in Dinosaur Town?' he said. 'Couldn't be better. We've made our way through the lava plain and on to the deserted city.' His eyes narrowed. 'How do you know about our game?'

'I was chatting to Samantha at the bakery.' The goth girl worked behind the counter on weekends. Her black hair, pale skin, and ruby red lips made her look more like someone who should have been drinking the blood of people at night rather than working behind the counter of a bread shop. She'd said she met with Jim and the others to play on Saturday nights.

'She was saying she liked the game.'

'Really?'

Jim looked pleased. So pleased that it confirmed an idea that I had been harbouring for some time: he had a massive crush on Sam. I had no idea how such a relationship would work out. He was tall, conservative, and geeky, while she was short, radical, and...well, also geeky.

Anyway, it wasn't my place to interfere in his love life; I couldn't even fix my own. Thanking him, I was considering hanging around for a while longer when my phone rang. It was Harry calling. Slowly making my way back to my car, I gave him a summary of what I'd discovered. I also sent him the pictures I'd taken, and he said they'd update the website.

'That's good work,' he said. 'By the way, I've got another lead for you.'

'Something good?'

'Rubbish dumping.'

'Oh great.'

He chuckled over the phone. 'Don't be like that,' he said. 'People love getting up in arms about rubbish being dumped in bushland.'

I agreed it was an issue, but a stepdown from a body on a beach. Harry gave me the location, and I was soon back in my car with Trixie at my side.

'Looks like we're off to the park,' I said.

Trixie gave a bark as she looked out the window. Parks were always good. Soon, we were pulling off the Great Coastal Road at Hansom Bay and into the Blackwood National Park.

I inhaled deeply. It was lovely here, but I particularly liked it after rain. It seemed to bring the bush to life.

A journey down a winding road brought us to Lakey Falls.

This is beautiful, I thought, as I got out of my car. *I can't see why anyone would ever want to ruin this by dumping rubbish.*

According to Harry, the rubbish had been tossed somewhere close to the parking lot. The falls were about half a kilometre down another trail. There were a couple of other vehicles in the car park, but they were empty. Walking the circumference of the car park, it only took me a few minutes to find the dumping spot.

Someone had tossed a suitcase full of belongings over the edge. I peered down the slope. There was clothing and a—

My foot gave way on the loose soil, and I went tumbling down the incline. Desperately trying to grab something on the way down, my hands raked the undergrowth as I slid down the bushy hillside. I glimpsed ferns and trees. Patches of sky. More trees. Finally, I came to a halt, my legs pointed up the slope. Stunned, I became aware of Trixie's distant frenzied barking.

An elderly man's head appeared over the edge. 'My dear!' he called. 'Are you all right?'

Sure! I do this all the time!

'I'm okay,' I said, trying to regain some dignity. Scrambling about to get more traction on the slope, I saw there was a sheer drop another ten metres below me. Judging by the sound of the gushing water, I suspected the river leading to the waterfall was about fifty metres below that. I'd been lucky, all things considered. A fall over the side may not have been survivable.

Fortunately, I'd landed close to the bag of junk that the dumper had discarded. He'd likely hoped to get it over the edge but failed.

Groaning, I checked my body. There'd be bruises. And lots of them.

'Should I call someone?' the man yelled.

'No. No, I'm fine.'

'I can get the SES. Or the fire brigade.'

Getting the fireys out here wasn't a bad option. Eye candy would go some way in alleviating my pain.

Trixie gave a bark.

Maybe she was reading my mind.

'No,' I called to the man. 'I'm fine.'

'I've got a tow bar,' the man offered. 'I can hitch a rope to you and pull you up.'

The man was obviously trying to be helpful, but being compared to a dumped vehicle was no good for my ego. 'I'll make my own way up,' I said. 'Thanks.'

He continued to speak as I glanced over at the scattered

possessions. It appeared to be women's clothing. And there was the suitcase—

Wait a minute...

The suitcase looked familiar—and I knew why. I'd seen it back at the Seaview. *These are the belongings the man took from the hotel!* Carefully navigating the undergrowth, I scooped up the clothing and other possessions and jammed them into the suitcase.

Slowly ascending the slope, I was nearly at the top when a rope came flying over the edge and hit me in the head. The elderly man appeared again.

'Sorry,' he said.

'It's fine.'

I gripped the rope and used it to drag myself up the last few metres. The man looked me up and down. 'Goodness,' he said. 'You took quite a tumble.'

I'd put on one of my suit combos that morning: a navy-grey skirt and jacket. Now, the skirt was torn and the jacket was smeared green and brown. Even a visit to the dry-cleaners wouldn't save this outfit.

'Are you sure you're fine?' the man asked.

I looked down at the suitcase in my hand. 'I'm fine,' I said. 'Perfectly fine.'

21

'Good Lord!' Harry said. 'What happened to you?' He held up a hand. 'No, don't tell me. You fell over.'

'I did,' I said. 'But it was completely worth it.'

Plonking the suitcase onto Harry's desk, everyone in the office crowded around to hear the story. Doris, Ellie, and Jay were sympathetic, and Harry—to his credit—managed not to laugh. He's a wonderful guy but has always taken great delight in my clumsiness.

'When I got back to the car,' I said. 'I searched the bag for identification. There was nothing—at first. But then I found an old receipt tucked into a side pocket in the name of S. Russo.'

'S. Russo?' Harry said.

'*Sofia Russo,*' I said, not able to keep the note of triumph from my voice. 'She was the maid at the Bailey house.' My mind had been ticking over since I'd discovered her name. 'Edna Crayborne was right. She saw a murder. It was Sofia.

The woman was obviously killed at the Bailey house and her body moved later.'

'Okay,' Harry said, holding up a hand. 'I've heard enough. Everyone skedaddle except for Rosie.' The office cleared, and Harry gently closed his door to give us some privacy. He sat down in his chair and faced me. 'We need to talk.'

'About what?'

'About what you're getting yourself into. One murdered woman is enough. We don't want another—and we especially don't want it to be you.'

'I'm fine.'

'This has all the makings of a big story,' he said. 'But there's more. I had a call from Lily Bailey this morning.'

'And?'

'She's threatening to sue us over that story. Lily's saying you made up your little ghost story just to sell papers.'

'I would never—'

Harry held up a hand. 'I know you didn't make it up,' he said. 'And people are always threatening to sue us. It comes with the territory. But I want to make sure that you're fine to keep pursuing this.'

'What do you mean?'

'Rosie,' he said. 'If there's a killer on the loose, your life could be at risk.'

I thought about Nan and Amanda and Tom. And Trixie.

Then the woman on the beach. The way the wind had peeled back the sheet, uncovering her lifeless body.

'Harry,' I said. 'An innocent woman has been killed. I doubt the killer would ever come after me or my family, but we can take precautions.'

'Such as?'

'The police.'

'I heard we've got a new sergeant. Is he any good?'

I decided not to mention that I'd just been on a date with him. 'He's okay,' I said. 'He's not used to the way we do things around here.'

Harry nodded. 'That does take some getting used to.'

'I'll be fine,' I said. 'And risk comes with the territory.'

'It could be an idea to drop in on John Bailey. You haven't spoken to him yet about what happened at the house. And he hasn't threatened to sue us. He might see things differently to his sister.'

It seemed like a good idea. 'I'll do that. Anything else?'

'Just promise you'll be careful.'

'I promise.'

Lugging the bag back to my desk, I quickly called Todd and told him what I'd found. Although he was dubious at first, he soon realised I was onto something when I mentioned the woman had worked at the Bailey house.

'Well done,' he said. 'That's going to help a lot.'

I told him he was welcome, and that I'd leave the bag in the office for him to collect. Hanging up, I searched on the net for the location of John Bailey's business. I suspected that Harry was right. John might know something more about what happened the night of his parents' murders. He may well add something to the official story.

Heading off home, I quickly got changed and patched my wounds. Nan, of course, asked me what had happened, and I told her.

'Clumsiness runs in the Ryan family,' she said. 'Don't forget about Greg's leg.'

I groaned. 'Nan,' I said. 'Not Greg's leg. Not again.'

'Yes! Greg's leg!'

The whole incident was tragic-funny. I'd mistakenly told Kim the story one Saturday over a bottle of red wine, and we'd ended up on the floor in hysterics.

'That boy would be walking on two legs if only he'd been nimbler,' Nan said. 'And watched where he was going.'

Poor cousin Greg had visited a wildlife park on the Gold Coast when he slipped and fell into the crocodile enclosure. It had only taken an instant for a crocodile to latch onto his leg. Good thing there was a passing Japanese tour bus. The tourists had risked life and limb to drag Greg clear. He survived the experience—minus one of his legs—but it showed that the clumsiness gene could cause lasting damage.

'I'll be careful,' I said.

It seemed I was saying that a lot lately.

After applying some Mercurochrome and bandages, I returned to my car with Trixie, and we hit the road. I was feeling better despite my injuries. Edna's claim that there had been a murder was correct. The victim was Sofia Russo. How she slotted into the deaths of the Baileys was unknown, but at least we now knew her name.

John Bailey lived in Forrest, a tiny town forty minutes' drive from the coast. Along the way, we passed vast swathes of undulating green hills, dotted with sheep and cattle. The animals stood about sedately as Trixie and I passed. She occasionally woofed at them.

'I agree,' I said to her, laughing. '*Woof! Woof!*'

Reaching Forrest, I first enjoyed a quick meal in a local café before going to John's place. It turned out to be a shopfront at the end of the main road. The place looked like it had once been a bookstore, but now it was *Bailey's Audio and Video Den*. Behind the store was a stately Georgian-style timber place. It looked impressive. I suspected that John lived there.

Looks like he's doing better than his sister, I thought.

Pushing open the front door, I stepped in to see a workshop lined with shelves packed full of old video and audio players. I'd thought the place looked a bit dusty from the outside, but inside, it was more like walking into a museum. I hadn't seen technology like this for years. Some items I'd only ever seen in pictures on the internet.

There was the rustle of feet from a backroom, and then John appeared. His expression turned into a grin.

'Oh,' he said. 'It's you.'

'John,' I said. 'I came here to apologise for the article. It didn't quite turn out the way I was expecting.'

'Don't worry about it,' John said. 'Lily's furious, but it really makes no difference to me. I just like my privacy. Every time something like this comes up, people in the town look at me a little differently. Then things eventually calm down, and life returns to normal.'

'Anyway,' I said. 'I'm sorry.'

He offered me a glass of water. I took a long sip and pointed to the equipment. 'This is a fantastic collection,' I said. 'Are these for sale, or do you use them for your video transfer?'

'Both,' he said. 'It's all for sale if someone's prepared to pay the price.'

'Some of it's quite pricy?'

He pointed out a few pieces. Some were valued at several thousand dollars. It surprised me. I had no idea there was a market for such things.

'There's been a lot of interest in the house,' I said, gradually bringing the conversation back to the purpose of my visit. 'I'm hoping to speak to everyone connected with the deaths. James

Nelson and Giuseppe Costa, and the staff.'

'Okay,' John said. 'Well, James Nelson and Giuseppe Costa both live in Cape Carson. So does Wayne Price. I think he works at that burger place. The difficult one to track down might be Sofia Russo. She moved away. I don't know where she's gone.'

An image of the woman's body on the beach flashed through my mind.

I know where she is, I thought. *The Cape Carson morgue.*

'Do you have any thoughts about the third bullet?' I asked.

John laughed. 'That's easy to explain,' he said. 'There was no third bullet. There were only two shots.'

'Lily thought there were three.'

'She was always in her room talking to friends on the phone,' John said. 'I don't know how she heard anything.'

'And where were you?'

'In the kitchen with Wayne and Sofia.'

'So you're not aware of anything suspicious in connection with your parents' deaths?'

'Well,' he considered. 'There are some things I could say, but it's best if I don't.' He hesitated. 'Although, you know I mentioned Wayne a moment ago?'

'Yes.'

'I never trusted him.'

'Why?'

John bit his lip. 'Because he was fixated with my mother.'

'Fixated?' I said. This was news. 'You mean Wayne was in love with her?'

'More than that. You could see it in his face every time she entered the room. I heard him speaking to Sofia one day. He said he'd marry her if he could.'

This put a different complexion on things. I'd known Wayne slightly for years. Ever since I started going to Sandy's Diner. He could have been in love with Claire. After all, these things happened.

'But why kill your mother?' I asked.

'I don't know, but there was a raging argument between my father and Wayne that afternoon.'

'Really?'

'Something to do with wages. At least, that was the official story. I'm sure it had something to do with my mother. I heard them speaking, and Wayne was saying he didn't like the way she was being treated.'

'So Wayne could have gone to the attic later—'

'—and confronted my father,' John said. 'Wayne could have shot Dad and also Mum if she tried to intervene.'

I nodded thoughtfully. Unrequited love affairs happened all the time. Except, this didn't gel with the facts. Everyone was downstairs when they heard the shots. Wayne could have paid for someone to kill the Baileys. He was the first one to enter the attic. He could have raced down the secret staircase and relocked the door after them.

I thought about the affable guy I'd seen at Sandy's over the years. Although I hadn't known him well, I'd never thought any ill of him.

Was it possible he was a murderer?

'There's something else,' John Bailey continued.

'What?'

John shook his head. 'I shouldn't even mention this,' he said. 'I love my sister, and I'd do anything for her. It's just that Lily was always—how can I put it—high strung. She used to get terribly angry, no, *furious*, when we were kids. It was something to see.'

'You think she had something to do with your parents' deaths?'

'No,' John said firmly. 'Well...I can't believe she would have. It's just that Lily would scream and throw things. I've never seen anyone with such a terrible temper in my life.'

That tied in with what Mina from the library had said.

John continued. 'I'll never forget something she said after our parents were killed. We came back from the funeral and were clearing out our rooms. After a while, I went in to see Lily. She was standing stock-still in the middle of her room, so I asked if she was okay.'

'What did she say?'

'Lily said she was fine. Better than she'd been for a long time. I said I found that hard to believe.' He shuddered. 'And you know what she did? She smiled, and it was like looking at someone I'd never seen before. Then she said, *I'm glad Mum and Dad are dead. I wish they'd died years ago.*'

22

My mind was busy as I drove back to Cape Carson, but my body knew I'd been through a tough time when I got out of my jeep.

I groaned. *Oh boy. I'm not as young as I used to be.* My body ached in a dozen places from my tumble down the slope in the national park. Moving like a geriatric, I made my way into the office.

Doris glanced up from her computer. 'You look awful.'

'That's great, Doris. Thanks for your honest opinion.'

You could always rely on Doris to tell you the truth.

The woman pushed back her glasses. 'You're welcome,' she said. 'You need to lie down and let your body recover.'

Harry leaned from his office and surveyed me. 'Doris is right,' he said. 'You look like you've spent the weekend at a dance marathon. Go home. Sleep. Recover. We'll see you tomorrow.'

I reluctantly agreed. After filling Harry in on what John

Bailey had said, I returned to the car and drove home. Trixie stuck by me as I hobbled inside to find Nan on the lounge working on the memory quilt. It was finally taking shape. Most sections had been attached, and she was adding the finishing touches.

Nan glanced up at me. 'You're falling apart at the seams, Rosie,' she said. 'You should do yoga with me in the mornings.'

'Sure. I always wanted to be a human pretzel.'

I took painkillers and decided to get some sleep. Getting into bed, Trixie hopped up next to me. I rarely allowed her onto the bed, but I was in no mood to protest.

'You're a naughty dog,' I said, stroking her neck. 'You're a very naughty....'

That's when sleep came.

Kra-ack!

I opened my eyes, confused about where I was and what was happening. Was I supposed to be at work? Had I slept in? What time was it? My eyes found the face of my digital clock.

3:10

Groaning, I lay back. It was still the middle of the night. Lightning flashed across the ceiling of my room. It was raining outside and blowing a gale. It sounded like the storms that had been lashing the coast were back.

The trees outside were whooshing about in a frenzy, like clothes in a washing machine. And something was banging.

What's that sound?

I climbed out of bed and stumbled down the hallway. More lightning flashed, bathing the living room in iridescent light.

Where's that noise coming from?

My eyes searched the shadows. A floorboard creaked to my left. A figure loomed in the dark.

I screamed.

They screamed.

We both screamed.

'Heavens!' Nan yelled. 'What are you doing?'

'Screaming!' I hissed, noticing Nan was wielding something overhead. 'What is that?'

'A golf club. I felt like a round.'

'Well, watch what you hit with that.'

We crossed to the window and peered out. A nearby street-light bathed the wet road in a white-hot glare. Leaves and branches were sailing about, driven by the wind. Beyond the streetlight lay inky blackness.

The banging came again.

'That's from the garage,' Nan said.

'I'll check it out.'

'I'm going with you.'

I recognised that determined expression. Nan had the same look when she said things like, *I'm starting tennis lessons,* and *I might try parachuting.*

'It might not be safe,' I said.

'No burglar's going to scare me!'

We crept down the internal stairs. A breeze pushed at my face as I shoved the door open to the garage. Nan raised the golf club. I snapped on the light. My eyes swept the chamber: car, bench, bicycle, tools.

Window. A torrent of cold air was rushing through the smashed window. A branch protruded through the pane.

'Must have come off a tree,' I said.

'Suppose so.'

I checked the garage door. It was still secured, and there was a deadlock on the inside. The only way someone was getting in was with a sledgehammer.

'Not much we can do tonight,' I said, eyeing the damage. 'I'll get a repairman tomorrow.'

I led Nan upstairs. She was calmer now but still determined to take the nine-iron to bed with her. I returned to the living room, snapped off the light, and peered out once more into the darkness.

The brake lights of a vehicle flared in the night and disappeared around the corner. My hands were shaking as I rechecked all the locks before returning to bed. Lying in the dark, I stared up at the ceiling. *Had someone been trying to break in? Could it be the killer?* Maybe my snooping around had gotten their attention.

I didn't feel like I was any closer to discovering who had killed Sofia Russo or what really happened to the Baileys, but the killer didn't know that.

The next day, I awoke feeling sore and sorry for myself. My leg ached badly, and I was coming out all over in bruises. After showering, I grabbed a quick breakfast and went for a walk with Trixie down to the beach. There were broken branches and leaves everywhere after the wild storm.

The morning was still cold, and the wind pulled at my hair as I marched resolutely up the beachside towards the lighthouse.

Trixie loved it. We passed a couple we knew who owned a poodle, and she let out a happy bark in greeting. Giving her a doggy snack, I peered up ahead to see Amanda's husband, Tom, heading towards me.

'Morning, Tom,' I said. 'You're out early.'

'I couldn't sleep last night because of the storm.'

I remembered the woman he'd met earlier in the week. There was no good way to mention her without accusing Tom of having an affair. Instead, I told him about the broken window and asked if he'd noticed anything odd in the street.

'Odd?' Tom said. 'You mean like a burglar?'

'Something like that.'

'We don't get too many burglaries around here.'

'Not many.'

He said neither he nor Amanda had seen or heard anything.

'I'd better get moving,' he said, glancing at his watch. 'There's a handyman we use for rental properties. I'll get him to drop by your place later and fix that window.'

'I think we'll have extra locks installed as well,' I said. 'On all the doors and windows.'

'I'm sure he can do that.'

I continued towards the lighthouse. It's always been one of my favourite walks. The Cape Carson lighthouse is undoubtedly our leading tourist attraction. The hundred-foot-high tower is white with red stripes around the gallery and over a century old. The nearby Lighthouse Inn is an equally iconic building, an old granite structure nestled in a shallow glade among overhanging eucalypts.

The final walk up to the lighthouse is relatively steep, but it's worth every step. The view from its base is glorious. You can see all the way up and down the coast. I leaned on the railing, enjoying the brisk air that pushed at my face as I tried to put everything together that had happened.

First, there was the mystery of the three gunshots. Or two depending on who you believed. Then there was Sofia Russo. What was she doing back at the Bailey house? And who would have murdered her?

And why? And did someone try to break into our place last night? Or was the branch through the window just an unlucky coincidence?

And, then, what about Wayne? John Bailey had raised some interesting questions about him. Is it possible that Wayne's argument with the Baileys led to their deaths?

I had plenty of questions and no answers. I glanced at my watch. I'd better get moving. Otherwise, I'd be late getting to my meeting with James Nelson. Heading back home, I grabbed the car and Trixie and I drove down the coast to where he lived.

Nelson's home was set back high on a hill overlooking the ocean, invisible to anyone driving along the Great Coastal Road. Getting to it meant turning off the road and onto a dirt driveway that curved around the steep hill.

The driveway opened out onto a wide parking area. Beyond it stood a modern single-story house made with steel uprights and huge glass windows. It was the sort of place an architect would own. Simple and striking. And expensive too. He'd obviously done well out of designing other people's homes. A BMW was parked at a jaunty angle in the driveway as if ready for a magazine photoshoot.

I shook my head as Trixie and I climbed from the car. 'I knew journalism was a dead-end,' I muttered. Trixie barked and gave me a reproachful look, so I gave her a doggy snack. 'Relax. You know I'm not serious.'

Glancing out to sea, I saw a freighter and a few sailing ships a long way off the coast. The view from here was spectacular though the onshore winds must have been ferocious. Even now, it was cold and windy. I suppose the place had the best heating and insulation that money could buy. You'd need it up here.

None of that meant anything, however, if you left your front door wide open. And this was precisely what James Nelson had done.

'Hello?' I said, leaning into a minimalistic concrete hallway. 'James Nelson? Are you home?'

Silence greeted me.

The man could have had a medical episode. He'd sounded elderly on the phone. I continued into the combined living room-kitchen and found it similar to the hall. More concrete, some stainless steel, and a few sparse decorations.

'James Nelson?' I called.

More silence.

I crept from room to room. There didn't appear to be anything amiss. Glancing into his office revealed nothing special: an architect's desk near the window and low, flat filing cabinets that would have contained architectural drawings.

A computer monitor sat on another desk. It all looked very neat and orderly.

Heading to the rear of the building, I found the back door open. *This is strange.* The man's house was empty, and he was nowhere to be found. Leaving through the back door, I wandered over to the edge and peered down. It was a sheer drop all the way around the property.

My eyes followed the base of the cliff as it receded back into a narrow gorge. An odd shape lay at the bottom. It was as if a bundle of clothing had been dumped off the edge. But it wasn't a bundle of clothing.

It was the body of James Nelson.

23

'This is becoming a habit,' Kim said.

'Two dead bodies in one week are two, too many,' I agreed.

We were in the living room at my place. Nan and I were working on the memory quilt while Kim thoughtfully sipped her hot chocolate. It had been a long day. After the police had turned up, I'd been quizzed before going back to the station to answer more questions. It had been nice seeing Todd again, but he was all business and no play. He had confirmed something, though: the body on the beach was Sofia Russo, and she'd been staying in the Seaview Hotel.

Her reason for returning to Cape Carson was unknown. Todd had refused to tell me if they were taking Edna's story any more seriously. Although, later, when I drove past the Bailey house, a cop car was parked out the front. That couldn't be a coincidence.

I'd tried asking Todd a few questions, but he refused to say anything. The rest of my day had been spent following up on other stories at the office.

I peered into the darkness outside the house. It had stopped raining again, and the night was clear and dry.

'They've got to be connected,' Nan said, stitching a section of cloth that had a laser jet-printed image of the town map onto the quilt. We'd coloured in the spot where Nan and Frank used to run the post office. 'So whoever killed that Russo woman also murdered the architect.'

'If he was killed,' Kim said. 'There's no evidence of that.'

I shook my head. 'Two people who were in the house the night the Baileys were killed happen to die within a few days of each other?' I said. 'That's no coincidence.'

'Then James Nelson must have known something.'

'Kim's right,' Nan said, looking up from the quilt. 'Didn't you mention that James Nelson said he knew something about the Baileys?'

The architect's words ran through my mind.

I've got some things to say about the Bailey house.

'Sofia Russo was the maid,' I said. 'James Nelson designed the place. Could there be a serial killer in Cape Carson? Someone picking off anyone associated with the house?' The idea had been lurking in the back of my mind all day. 'But that doesn't explain why Sofia was at the house.'

'She must have been meeting someone there,' Nan said. She was finished with the transfer now and was attaching a sleeve to the quilt. 'Someone she knew from the old days.'

'There's someone else I still need to speak to about the case,' I said. 'Giuseppe Costa.'

'That blowhard?'

'I'm afraid so.' Giuseppe Costa was renowned for having what could euphemistically be called a *big personality*. 'His life could be in danger. He should at least be warned.'

'I hear he's got lots of enemies,' Nan said.

'I'll visit him,' I said, adding in my best Godfather voice, '*I'm gonna make him an offer he can't refuse.*'

Laughing, Kim and I went onto the veranda to enjoy the evening. The temperature had turned warm again after all the rain of the last few days. It sounded like people were making the most of it. From somewhere down the street came the sound of laughter. Someone was having a barbeque. A shape moved in a nearby tree.

'Is that Possy?' Kim asked.

Possy was the ringtail possum that lived in the tree beside our house. I peered up into the branches. 'I'm pretty sure that's him,' I said. Having a wild animal as a neighbour had its ups and downs. We loved having him, but he ate everything in sight. The apple tree in the backyard had a net over it to keep him away from the fruit. 'Maybe he's going to the barbeque.'

'Could be a gate crasher,' Kim agreed and turned to me. 'Rosie, are you sure you're safe here?'

'We're fine.'

'So that branch smashing through your window was just a coincidence?'

'We're in the middle of suburbia,' I said. 'The window's been fixed, and I've had extra locks put on all the doors and windows.' I turned to her. 'You suddenly seem very concerned about my wellbeing. What about *Ideally Yours*?'

'What about it?'

'Sending your best friend off on dates with complete strangers hardly seems safe.'

'It's safe enough. But it sounds like you've been doing okay without it.' She lowered her voice. 'Tell me about Todd.'

'There's nothing to tell.'

'Really? Your eyes go all goo-goo whenever I mention his name.'

'They do not!'

Kim looked dreamy. 'I think you've got one on the line.'

'Huh?'

'You've just got to reel him in!'

'You're a crazy person! I barely know the guy!'

'I can hear wedding bells.'

'You're hearing bells because you're a ding-dong!'

The screen door slid across, and Nan appeared. 'Hey Kim,' she said. 'You asking Rosie about Todd?'

'Sure am.'

Nan nodded knowingly. 'Rosie gets a funny look whenever she talks about him,' she said. 'She's love drunk. Doesn't take a psychic to know they'll get married. I've already booked the venue. Get your tickets now while they're cheap.'

Nan and Kim were so ridiculous that I burst out laughing. I heard Possy scamper away into the branches of a darkened tree. 'You're both crazy!' I yelled. 'Stark raving mad!'

'Maybe,' Kim said. 'But it doesn't mean we're wrong.'

That night I slept with no problems. There were no broken windows or raging storms.

The following day I took Trixie out and did the bay walk from end to end, passing tourists and joggers as we went. Reaching Cut Rock lookout, I saw someone heading towards me with a familiar-looking greyhound.

'Hey you,' Todd said.

'Hey yourself,' I replied. I remembered what Nan and Kim had said about me looking weird whenever I mentioned Todd, so I did my best to remain stony-faced.

'Everything okay?' he asked.

'Oh! Sure!' My focus changed to his body, and I realised he must have already completed a morning workout. If anything ever happened between us—and it was a big if—I wondered how double-shot caramel latte Rosie would keep up with him. Todd was strong. He could toss me around like a human beachball, whereas I had problems picking up my bag some days.

However, he obviously loved fitness—and I loved guys who looked fit! Surely that counted for something!

'Any movement on the case?' I asked.

He sighed. 'You know I can't talk about an active case.'

'Two heads are better than one.'

I fluttered my eyes at him.

'Are you fluttering your eyes?' he asked.

'Just something in them. Might be sand.' I persevered. 'It's obvious the two murders are linked. Sofia worked at the Bailey house, and James Nelson designed it.'

'There's another link to be considered.'

'And that is?'

'You've visited both crime scenes.'

'*I'm a suspect?*'

'Maybe I should bring you in for questioning.'

'For what reason?'

'I'm not sure,' Todd said, trying to stifle a grin. 'Could be your dress style.'

'My dress style—' My mind returned to the restaurant, and I remembered the way he was staring at my dress. 'You—idiot! You knew my dress was on backward!'

'The label at the front was a dead giveaway.'

'And you didn't say anything!'

'I thought you always dressed like that.'

I hit his shoulder—hard. Unsure if I wanted to yell at him or burst out laughing, I instead marched off with Trixie trailing after me. I was sure I could still hear Todd chuckling all the way home.

Later, once I got to the office, I rang Giuseppe Costa's office to make an appointment to see him. Fortunately, he had some time free, and his secretary slotted me in. I worked on an article about some upcoming roadworks until Ellie approached me.

'I've found some old images of the Bailey place,' she said. 'You might be interested in seeing them.'

She plugged a memory drive into my laptop.

'Are these copies of old editions?' I asked.

One of Ellie's roles was to digitise the back issues of the newspaper. It was a time-consuming process but a vital one to help people interested in the town's history.

'No,' she said. 'These are old crime scene pictures.'

'Really? How did we get those?'

'Harry said he 'acquired' them after the murders happened. He wasn't able to do anything with them because it would have meant revealing a source within the police department.'

Ellie opened the files. They weren't gruesome, something for which I was grateful. The pictures had been taken just after Justin and Claire had died, although their bodies had been taken away. One of the pictures grabbed my attention. It had been taken from a similar angle to the lifestyle photoshoot the paper had run just before their deaths.

My eyes focused on Stanley, the bird.

You poor thing, I thought.

Stanley must have flown about wildly when the gun went off. His feathers were all over the floor. I remembered the stray feathers Kim and I had found in the attic.

My eyes scanned the pictures again. A niggling feeling churned in my gut. There was something strange about the images though what that was, I had no idea.

What is it?

Copying the pictures to my backup drive would allow me to recheck them later. I thanked Ellie and checked my watch.

'I've got to get moving,' I said. 'Giuseppe Costa doesn't like to be kept waiting.'

Heading down the main road, I passed Tom and Amanda's business and glanced inside. Amanda was sitting on the edge of Tom's desk as they discussed something on his computer. I remembered his meeting with the woman and how my own marriage had ended so unhappily. My heart ached.

I hope all's well in paradise.

Giuseppe's office was on the first floor of a building on Percy Street. The view overlooked the whole of Cape Carson beach. Not that the secretary got to enjoy it much. Her desk was strategically turned away, so she had her back to the window. I'd met her a few times over the years. She was an older, gaunt woman named Teresa, a retired schoolteacher, and probably handpicked by Giuseppe's wife, Sharon, to keep him in hand.

Among his many less admirable qualities, Giuseppe was a notorious womaniser.

I was only sitting in the waiting room for a few minutes when voices were raised on the other side of Giuseppe's door. It sounded like he was arguing with a woman. Then something was broken. The door was thrown open, and Sharon Costa appeared. She was as tall as me, buxom with a Grecian nose, blonde hair, and high cheeks. Those cheeks were presently flaming red.

'Rosie,' she said, stopping in surprise. 'What are you doing here?'

I glanced past her into the office and spotted a broken vase on the floor. 'Interviewing your husband,' I said. 'I hope.'

'You can have him! He's more trouble than he's worth.'

Upon saying this, she stormed down the stairs. Giuseppe appeared in the doorway. He seemed absolutely nonplussed, considering he'd just had a raging argument with his wife.

'Rosie Ryan!' he said, flinging open his door. 'Come in! Come in!'

I followed him inside and sat in a seat opposite. Unlike the reception area, his desk faced the ocean while I had a view of the wall behind him. There were plaques everywhere, mostly civic awards that the Cape Carson Business Council handed out.

They didn't mean a whole lot.

A few were from Rotary and the Lions Club. Maybe Giuseppe had made some tax-deductible donations.

'I hope I'm not interrupting anything,' I said.

'What? You mean Sharon?' He laughed. 'She's high-strung. You know what women are like.'

I had some idea, being one myself, but now wasn't the time to debate his views of women. I'd heard him mentioned in connection with three other females around town. For some reason, though, Sharon stayed with him. She was either dumb, patient, or they had some kind of agreement.

It made me wonder what anyone saw in him. Giuseppe was a short, chubby man, clean-shaven with a bad combover. He wore a grey suit and a big gold ring on his wedding finger. Had someone told me he was a used car salesman, it wouldn't have surprised me.

I told Giuseppe the purpose of my visit.

His face fell. 'I see,' he said. 'The Bailey house. Yeah, I saw that article. I was hoping you were here to ask me about the new eco-resort.'

'Eco-resort?'

'Sand Palace on West Beach.'

I knew all about Sand Palace. There'd been a lot of fanfare about it, particularly from Giuseppe himself. What he saw as an eco-resort, most other people saw as another ugly hotel complex. His plan was to build a massive resort on the seven miles of undeveloped coastline to the west of town. With the council already voting against it twice, the chances of it ever being built were almost zero.

'No,' I said. 'I'm hoping you can tell me about the Baileys and the night they died.'

'That was a long time ago. I'm not sure there's much I can say.'

'Whatever you can remember would be helpful. I understand you were in business with Justin Bailey.'

'Not business. Not even close. No, Justin owned a piece of land I was interested in. I'd been trying to encourage him to sell it, or even for us to become partners, so we could bring our dream to fruition.'

It sounded more like Giuseppe's dream than Justin's. 'Where's this piece of land?' I asked.

'Northville.'

I frowned. 'Where the winery is?'

He nodded. 'With a bit of work, that whole area could have been developed into a housing estate,' he said. 'Hundreds of homes. A new town. It's not every day you get to do that.'

'Have you approached Lily about the land?'

'She's not interested.' Giuseppe looked down at his nails. 'Wants to grow grapes. I understand people wanting to do things themselves.' He picked up a clear dome-shaped paper-weight. A twenty-dollar note had been encased in clear resin. 'This was the first twenty dollars I earned. Made it mowing lawns. Now look where I am.'

Guiseppe's hard work was admirable, but I wasn't here to stroke his ego. 'Have you ever spoken to John about the land? Maybe he's a part-owner?'

'I don't think he is,' Guiseppe put down the weight. 'He's some kind of stockbroker. Plays the market and does pretty well out of it by all accounts.'

I nodded thoughtfully. 'I understand you were at the house the night the Baileys died?'

'I was supposed to be meeting Justin, though it was obvious he had other issues on his mind.' Giuseppe shook his head. 'I could hear him and his wife arguing. It went on for ages. Then there was complete silence for about an hour.'

'You waited an hour?'

'Like I said, I was interested in that land. Anyway, that's when I heard the shots.'

'How many shots?'

'Three.'

'You're sure about that?'

'Absolutely.' Giuseppe shrugged. 'I must have been asked about that a hundred times by the police. There were three shots. One, and then another two after it.'

'And what happened then?'

'At first, I didn't know what to do. Then I heard yelling, and I went racing into the hallway. I reached the bottom of the attic stairs with the staff and that architect...what's his name?'

'James Nelson.'

'That's right. Nelson.' Giuseppe frowned. 'Didn't he just kick the bucket?'

I nodded, not ready to dwell on that for the moment. 'And what happened next?'

'The cook went up the stairs first. It's the man who works at the horrible greasy spoon place in town.'

'Wayne from Sandy's Diner?' I said, annoyed that he was insulting my favourite eating place.

'That's it. Anyway, the cook broke the door down and found the bodies.' Giuseppe sighed. 'It was bad luck for everyone involved.'

Really? I thought. *Two people losing their lives is just bad luck?*

I resisted the urge to hurl the paperweight at his head.

'Can you think of anyone who would have wanted Justin and Claire dead?' I asked.

Giuseppe looked at me blankly. 'Enough to murder them?' he said. 'No. Definitely not Claire. She was a nice lady. A real looker, too. I don't know why she stayed with Justin. He was a drunk and an idiot. Should have stuck with his acting.'

'He was never actually an actor,' I pointed out.

'Yeah,' Giuseppe said, shrugging off the correction. 'But the theatre was his thing. He liked all the contraptions used to make the show happen: trap doors, backdrops, elevators.'

I thought of the secret passage Justin had built at the house. It tied in with his love of the theatre.

Giuseppe stroked his chin. 'I wonder if Justin missed his—what do you call it—vocation in life? He would have been better off keeping that theatre in Melbourne. Moving down here turned out to be the worst thing he could have done.'

We chatted for a while longer, but the property developer had nothing else to share. Standing to leave, I told him that James's death could be connected to another murder.

'So someone might be bumping off people linked to the house?' Giuseppe said, a crooked smile creasing his face. 'They don't want to muck around with me. They'd come out worse for wear.'

Nodding, I headed out the door.

I'm sure they would.

24

'Okay,' Kim said, leaning back in her seat. 'Let's go around and find out what you thought of *The Murder at Grimshaw Hall*.'

I glanced around at the other members of the Cape Carson Mystery Book Club. We were in one of the library meeting rooms, sitting around in a circle, as we always did, copies of our books in hand. Beyond the frosted glass windows, we could see people using the free computers or sitting around reading.

'Fabulous!' Nola Evans said.

'I read it on my new orange phone,' her twin sister Monica declared.

'Apple, Monica.'

'No, it's definitely orange.'

Nola and Monica were ninety-six years old. They were so identical to each other that I still got them mixed up. Birdlike with white hair and watery blue eyes, I had never seen the two women separate from each other. They came as a pair or not at all.

'One of Sherry Johnson's best,' Marlene Hogan joined in. She was a big woman with round fire engine framed glasses. As well as running the local sweet shop, she was a prolific reader, sometimes devouring up to five books a week. 'I never would have guessed the end.'

Wanda Gibson snorted.

All eyes turned to her. The Cape Carson Mystery Book Club was mostly an amiable group. I say *mostly* because there's always someone who likes to stir the pot, and that person in our group is Wanda Gibson. A woman of a certain age, give or take several more uncertain years, she dissected every mystery novel as surely as a scientist examining a cell under a microscope. Her brain was as sharp as cut glass and with good reason; before Kim, she'd worked as the head librarian for thirty years.

Wanda Gibson had grey, thinning hair and wore small round glasses. Her build was vaguely reminiscent of a bulldog. She didn't like people much—which she would gladly tell you to your face—and lived alone with her books and her cat, Bastet. The latter, she was famously known for taking on leashed walks through town. Despite her solitary nature, Wanda was an enthusiastic member of the club and a dozen other organisations around town.

The woman groaned. 'Come now,' Wanda said. 'The book contained the most preposterous method of murder that I've ever read. I mean, really, a heckelphone?' She turned to me. 'You're a discerning reader, Rosie. What did you think?'

'Oh well,' I said. 'Death by heckelphone? Yes, I suppose being...er, heckled to death...um....'

'You didn't read the book. Did you?'

'I didn't *quite* finish it.' Surely getting as far as chapter four qualified as not quite finishing. 'Is it obvious?'

'Very. A heckelphone is an orchestral instrument similar to an oboe.' Wanda turned to the others. 'I had the solution by Chapter Three. I knew Damien Rodan committed the crime. No one else could have done it.'

'What about the butler?' Edward Blayney asked.

Edward was a stout little man, balding, and the owner of Ed's Pastries and Cakes. He obviously ate too much of his own produce, but that could be easily excused. His unassuming shop, sandwiched between Dell's florist and the Cape Carson news agency, sold some of the best tarts and pies to be found anywhere on the Great Coastal Road. People were sometimes lined up down the block. I was continually amazed that he found any time for reading.

'The butler?' Wanda said icily. 'But the butler was in the living room when the murder happened.'

'I thought he may have been a twin.'

Now half the room groaned.

'Not a twin,' Nola Evans moaned.

'We get blamed for everything,' Monica Evans added.

Death by twin was never well received by the Cape Carson Mystery Book Club. A few other people had solutions to offer. One that was better received was from my office buddy, Doris Glow. She suggested the butler's son could have committed the crime. Even Wanda had to grudgingly admit it was possible, as the butler's son had a motive.

'Death by heckelphone is unique,' Monica spoke up, her plump face reddening. 'And although I don't think the twin hypothesis works,' another snort from Wanda, 'I do think the forged letter was a nice touch.'

I'd no idea there were so many fascinating elements in the novel, and I regretted not reading it.

'So who forged the letter?' Wanda demanded.

Monica thought for a moment. 'Alan?' she said, although it was clear even she didn't believe it.

Another snort followed, and there was silence until Doris spoke up.

'I liked the romance,' she said.

Oh yes, everyone enthused. We all liked the romance in the novel. Even me and I'd only made it as far as the fourth chapter. During the break, I corralled Kim in the corner, where we stood around with cream buns and tea and tried not to think of calories.

'I was sure the killer was the wife,' Kim said. 'Although

I thought the heckelphone was misdirection. I thought he might have been suffocated with a flute instead.'

'So the killer jammed a flute down his throat? Then removed it and suffocated him with the heckelphone?'

'That's about the long and the short of it.'

Doris wandered over. 'So you didn't finish the book?' she said, a faint smile on her lips. 'I don't think you missed a lot. It wasn't as good as her other book where the man is killed with a tuba.'

'Oh yes,' I said. 'Murder by tuba is so much easier to believe.'

Kim pointed to my top. 'Bad news, girlfriend,' she said. 'You've had an accident.'

I looked down and groaned. True to form, a chunk of cream had run a marathon down the front of my new blouse. Hastily wiping it away, I raced off to the bathroom to dab the rest out before it stained. Just as I was cleaning myself up, Wanda stormed into the bathroom and headed for the sinks.

'Ah, Rosie,' she said. 'Your article about the Bailey house was excellent.'

'Thanks.'

Praise from Wanda Gibson was rare.

'Your writing, that is,' she amended. 'Otherwise, Rosie, it was completely nonsensical. There are no such things as ghosts.'

'Okay,' I said, trying to keep my voice even. 'So, how do you explain the strange happenings?'

'I can't, but I'm wondering if you've spoken to Gabriel Jackson.'

Gabriel was a rough-looking woman I'd seen around town for years. I'd thought she was homeless until someone told me she worked as a barmaid at one of the local pubs.

'No,' I said. 'Should I?'

'Absolutely. She was Justin Bailey's mistress.'

'*What?*'

Wanda grinned at my expression. 'Oh yes,' she said. 'Gabriel and Justin used to regularly engage in, shall we say, recreational activities. My cousin Simon owned a tiny B&B near Barkly, and Justin used to take Gabriel there all the time.'

This was news. 'I had no idea that Justin had a mistress.'

'There may have been more than one. Simon's since passed away, but Justin and Gabriel became cockier as time went on. Justin would sneak Gabriel up those secret stairs, even when his wife was home.'

'What? That's awful,' I said. 'And you know about the secret staircase?'

'Half of Cape Carson knew about it.' Wanda finished washing her hands. 'Gabriel Jackson's still around. She works at the Smuggler's Inn. Talk to her.'

'I will.'

Thanking Wanda, I headed back to the meeting where the

next novel was announced: a classic mystery by Dorothy L Sayers.

Good, I thought. *I doubt Dorothy ever killed anyone with a musical instrument.*

Heading home, I found Nan still up and working on the memory quilt. Dave was there too, although his role seemed confined to supplying tea and biscuits. After finishing a line of stitches, Nan asked us to help her, and we laid the quilt out on the dining room table.

'My goodness,' Nan said. 'It's been a big project, but the quilt's almost done.'

I cast my eye over it. Pop's old shirts had been incorporated into the fabric, as had an old pair of his overalls. There were also handkerchiefs, ties, and even a hat he used to wear all the time. Lines of text had been sewn down the length of the pants.

'Is that some of Pop's poetry?' I asked.

Pop had written bush poetry as a form of recreation.

'It is,' Nan confirmed, glancing at her watch. 'I think it's time I did my walk around the block.'

'Do you want me to come with you?' Dave asked.

'You stay here. I need a few minutes to clear my head.'

She headed out the door, and I had a sip of Dave's tea.

Not bad, I thought.

'Do you mind if I ask about Frank?' Dave asked.

'What would you like to know?'

He rubbed his beard. 'What was he like?' he asked. 'I know Nan still misses him.'

'Pop was the greatest,' I said, settling into a seat opposite. 'Great sense of humour. Lots of energy. He and Nan ran the post office their whole lives.' I thought back to the man I knew. 'They were an institution here in Cape Carson. Had a lot of things he wanted to do when he retired, but it didn't quite work out that way.'

'I suppose they were pretty much tied to their business.'

'Yes—but no. Somehow they found time to drive around Australia three times.' I shook my head. 'I have no idea how they fitted it all in.'

'Nan mentioned he passed away only a few years ago.'

I nodded. 'Yeah,' I said. 'It was really sudden.'

Amanda and I had only been living with Nan and Pop for a few months. They had been talking non-stop about another trip around Australia. They would follow the coast around and visit all the places they hadn't been to yet.

Nan and Pop had been home alone that day. She'd gone out to do some shopping, but Pop stayed behind because he was tired and wanted to nap.

'It was me that found him,' I said to Dave. 'It was lucky, really. I came home because I'd forgotten my phone. Pop was asleep on the lounge. Or I thought he was. Then I saw how still he looked.' I shook my head. 'That's the thing I remember the most. He was always so animated. Always moving. I rang an ambulance, but it was too late. He'd died in his sleep. Heart attack, the doctors said.'

'You and Nan seem like a good team,' Dave said, running a hand through his beard. 'I hope you don't mind me dating her.'

'As long as your intentions are honourable.' I made a joke out of it, but I was also serious. 'She's a special lady.'

Dave smiled gently. 'My intentions are honourable,' he said. 'But Nan's the one to watch. She's got more get up and go than a kangaroo!'

25

I began the next day determined to interview Gabriel Jackson. Wanda had been right in saying she worked at the Smuggler's Inn. There are three watering holes in Cape Carson, which is quite a few when you consider the size of our town. Two are stylish and on the waterfront, and the third is the Smuggler's Inn. Set a street back from the main road, the place misses out on both the views and the tourists. It's mostly locals it attracts, and then it's locals who prefer their alcohol cheap.

Making my way into the pub, my eyes searched the gloomy interior for Gabriel. You'd think there'd be no one drinking in a pub at this time of the morning, but one determined guzzler was nursing his beer as he took in a thrilling view of the car park.

I finally spotted a woman at the other end of the bar. 'Gabriel?' I said, approaching.

She didn't look as bad as I expected, but she still didn't look good. Gabriel was probably forty but looked more like fifty.

Too many drinks after work had taken their toll. She was fleshy, with a pasty complexion, and her hair looked dry and in need of a cut. She'd probably been pretty once. It was a shame to see that she'd gone so downhill.

'Who wants to know?'

Her eyes lit up when I introduced myself. 'You're the one who wrote the ghost story in the paper,' she said. 'About Justin's place.'

'You knew Justin?' I said. 'And Claire?'

'I knew Justin better,' Gabriel said, smirking. 'We were friends back in the day.'

'More than friends, I've heard.'

The man nursing his drink finished and headed off, leaving the bar empty except for Gabriel and me.

'We shared some good times,' Gabriel said. 'But a lady doesn't kiss and tell.'

If you're a lady, then I'm a five-legged hippo.

I dove in. 'You were Justin's girl on the side,' I said. 'You two met at a B&B in the beginning. Then he showed you the secret staircase leading into the house.'

She frowned. 'You know about that?' she said. 'How?'

'I have my sources.'

'Then you probably know that Justin and I were going to get married,' she said. 'He was going to leave that wife of his and run off with me.'

'And when was that happening?'

'As soon as the right time came.'

I said nothing. It sounded like the oldest story in the book, like he'd led Gabriel on for his own benefit. Would he have ever left his wife? I wasn't sure how their finances were organised, but it may well have been a fifty-fifty split down the middle.

This made me think. If only Claire had been killed, then both Justin and Gabriel would have been the prime suspects. But that wasn't how it happened.

'Who else knew about the affair?' I asked.

'We kept it secret, but people knew.' Gabriel shrugged. 'It's hard to keep that sort of thing quiet.'

'And the secret passage?'

Gabriel laughed. 'Justin and I would synchronise watches,' she said. 'It was like a spy show. I'd come in the back gate, and he'd let me in via the secret entrance.'

'I know Justin and Claire drank. I've heard there were drugs as well.'

She shrugged. 'I don't know about that. It was straight-up Johnnie Walker for us.'

'Okay.'

The drugs might have been a new diversion.

I already knew the answer to my next question but asked it anyway. 'You couldn't let yourself in?'

'In through the secret door? No. There was a lock and a

latch. It could only be opened from the inside.'

I quizzed Gabriel for several more minutes, but it was clear she could shed nothing more about the events leading to Justin and Claire's deaths. Or Sofia Russo or James Nelson either. Gabriel said she didn't even know who they were. Thanking her, I headed back outside into the early morning sunshine. Trixie happily barked as I approached.

'You didn't think I'd leave you?' I said, untying her lead.

She barked again.

Returning to the office, I made notes and finished a story about an upcoming extension to the surf club. I had to leave work early; this was the night of Amanda's party.

Harry grumbled when I told him. He had a story he wanted me to start on: an exhibition at a local gallery.

'The exhibition's not starting till next week,' I said, studying the flyer he'd handed me. 'I can catch up with the gallery owners later.'

Harry sighed. 'Okay,' he said. 'Good thing you're my star reporter.'

'You're right about that.'

Heading back to my jeep, I was about to climb in when I spotted George walking up the hill.

'Hey Rosie,' he said. 'Looks like I was just in time.'

'Did you want to talk about something?'

'Just wanted to know when we should turn up.'

'Huh?'

'To the party,' he said. 'You know Blossom and I are coming? I saw Amanda the other day, and she said we could come.'

Oh great, I thought. *Just the people I wanted to see.*

I did my best to keep my face impassive, but it was hard. Seeing George was bearable. Having him flaunt about with Pumpkin Head at his side was the difficult bit. Unfortunately, I could hardly tell him not to come. He was Amanda's father, and I had no right to say he wasn't welcome.

'Of course,' I said. 'About seven o'clock should be fine. And just bring yourselves. I'm sure there'll be enough food to feed half of Cape Carson.'

I knew they'd bring something anyway, but that couldn't be helped. I headed home to find Nan already hard at work. Her stamina never failed to amaze me. It was hard to believe she was eighty-three. The kitchen was a battle zone with pots on the stove and pastries in the oven.

'You're just in time,' she said. 'I needed someone to make the rice salad.'

I'd long since learned that the kitchen was Nan's domain. Trying to give orders or take charge here was like trying to argue with a tidal wave.

'Then I'm your girl,' I said and got to work mixing ingredients.

Fortunately, I'd already put together Amanda's triple-layer

chocolate cake. By the time dinnertime arrived, we had food on tables on the veranda as visitors began to turn up. Amanda and Tom had gotten to know lots of people through their real estate dealings, and people piled in through the door at a rapid pace. Despite telling them not to bring anything, almost everyone brought an additional plate of food or a bottle of drink.

The music volume was turned up, and people started dancing. Fortunately, I'd picked the music and decided on disco. If people won't dance to YMCA, then they won't dance to anything. With the party in full swing, Kim helped me in the kitchen. 'There's a lot of people out there,' she said, grabbing another plate of fried chicken to feed the hungry masses.

'Feels like the whole town's here,' I agreed.

'Any more sausage rolls?'

'Right here.'

As the evening drew on, a few neighbours offered to take over the kitchen, allowing me to schmooze with the guests. It was my first time seeing the party at close hand. It looked like everyone was having a great time.

Well, almost everyone. I was surprised to see that George had turned up, but not Blossom.

'She couldn't make it?' I asked.

'Headache.'

I stared at him. There was something about the way he said

it that made me doubt he was telling the truth. Maybe they weren't getting on. Anyway, it was none of my business.

'Sorry to hear that,' I said.

Moving on, I saw an enormous figure appear at the front door, and I moved across to say hello.

'Glad you could make it,' I said.

Todd grinned. 'Wouldn't miss it for the world,' he said, waving a bottle of wine and a wrapped gift.

'You shouldn't have done that.'

'The gift was the hard part. It wasn't easy buying for some-one I don't know.'

'Then let's remedy that.'

I led him through the crowd to where Amanda and Tom were talking to a few friends.

'Ah, the famous Todd,' Amanda said after I introduced him. 'Mum's told me absolutely *nothing* about you.'

'There's *nothing* to tell,' I said. 'Now leave him alone. He's just walked in the door.'

Leading him away, I poured him a drink before we headed to the front veranda. A bunch of people were out there, chatting and laughing as the music wafted onto the street. I was a little concerned about the noise, but it was probably okay because most of our neighbours were at the party, anyway.

'So, how's the case going?' I asked.

'What case would that be?'

'Good question. Is it the mysterious deaths of Justin and Claire Bailey? Or the death of Sofia Russo? Or James Nelson? There's so many to pick from.'

'You know I can't comment on an ongoing investigation.'

'You can't do things alone in this town.' He didn't reply to this, but I could tell he was thinking about what I'd said, so I persevered. 'Do you know what Sofia was doing back in Cape Carson?'

'We haven't been able to establish a reason yet. Sofia has no family here. Her credit card records show she purchased a second phone some time back, but we have no record of the number.'

I thought hard. 'A burner phone,' I said. 'Sofia bought a phone that couldn't be traced. And she came here to Cape Carson to meet with someone.'

'That's a reasonable conclusion.'

'Then it must be in connection with the deaths at the Bailey house.'

Todd sighed. 'Rosie,' he said. 'I've looked into the deaths at the Bailey place, and there was nothing suspicious about them. It was a classic murder-suicide. Justin and his wife were heavy drinkers. There was an argument, and Justin killed his wife before taking his own life.'

'And what about the three gunshots?'

'Witnesses make mistakes all the time when it comes to

recalling events. Especially traumatic events. People thought they heard different things that night. There's nothing surprising about it. Besides,' he added, 'the door was locked from the inside. The cook had to break it down to gain entry.'

'What about the—'

'—secret passage? Yes, I know about that, and you probably also know that it was locked from the inside too. It was only Justin and Claire in that room. Oh, and the bird.'

That's right, I thought. *Spencer.*

A strange sensation tingled in the pit of my stomach.

There was something about Spencer and that murder scene. Something that wasn't right.

Tom stuck his head outside. 'Come on in, everyone,' he said. 'We're about to sing to the birthday girl.'

We all headed inside. I turned to Todd. 'I hope you're doing something about your eyesight,' I said.

'What are you now?' he asked with mock severity. 'My mother?'

'Just a concerned citizen. I don't want you shooting me in the butt by accident.'

I cast my gaze across the room—and stopped. There was a dark-haired woman I suddenly recognised.

That's the woman Tom was meeting!

Tom tapped a spoon against the side of a glass, and the crowd fell to silence.

'Thanks for coming,' he said. 'Amanda insisted she didn't want a party, but what kind of husband would I be if I listened to my wife?'

A titter of laugher rippled through the group.

'We also noted on the invitations that she didn't want any presents,' he continued, pointing to a pile of gifts in a corner. 'Looks like most of you are terrible at following instructions.'

More laughter.

'I was really stuck on what to get Amanda. She told me she has everything she needs. She lives in Cape Carson, which is the greatest place in the world. She has a wonderful mother and grandmother—plus, a pretty reasonable husband.'

Amanda drew close and gave him a hug. 'He's pretty okay,' she said.

There was a big *ooooh*.

'It's hard to get someone a present when they already have everything,' he said. 'So I decided to get Amanda something unique.' He nodded to the woman across the room. 'Abigail?'

The dark-haired woman picked up a flat rectangular object, and handed it to Amanda. Frowning, Amanda ripped it open and stared at the object as the wrapping paper fell away.

'Oh my goodness!' she gasped. 'It's beautiful!'

She turned it around and showed us a framed oil painting of Frank Ryan, my grandfather. It was new, so the artist must have worked off photos. They'd caught something in Frank's face. A cheekiness that he'd had in life. It was an amazing achievement.

'This is Abigail Wells,' Tom said, indicating the woman. 'She had to work on this in secret so Amanda wouldn't know.'

Everyone around me clapped as I slowly took in what had happened. Amanda had adored her great-grandfather, and his passing had really knocked her about. This was a fitting gift that would forever keep him in her memory.

Slowly, I put everything together. Tom had been meeting with the woman to secretly arrange Amanda's present. There was no affair. He had just wanted to do something special for his wife. I'd been a fool. Just because my own marriage had collapsed didn't mean that everyone else's was on the rocks. Tom and Amanda loved each other. They were as solid as concrete.

I began clapping too, louder than anyone else. 'Three cheers for Tom and Amanda!' I yelled. 'Hip! Hip! Hooray!'

26

'Ah-ha,' I said. 'That's interesting.'

'What is?' Jay asked.

After Amanda's party on Friday night, I'd spent the week-end catching up on household chores. For most of Monday morning, I'd sipped at my jumbo double-shot caramel latte while I whittled away at a story. Finally finishing it, I then turned to my growing inbox of unread emails.

'Hmm,' I said.

'Rosie?' Jay said.

I glanced over at him. Out of the corner of my eye, I'd noticed him frowning at his computer screen, trying to work out how to start a story he'd been given about the local soccer club.

'You first,' I said.

He groaned. 'The soccer club is starting a mixed team,' he said. 'I'm trying to think of a headline. Maybe about men and women working together.'

'That's hardly the lead,' I said. 'How about *Women Join the Ranks*?'

'You're the best,' he said, typing. 'So what's happening with you?'

The email I'd received was from someone named Doreen Hollis. 'She wants to talk to me about Sofia Russo's death,' I said. 'She knew Sofia from the old days.'

'Are you trying to dominate the front page again?'

'Absolutely.' That wasn't hard to do with me being one of the only two reporters in the office. 'I'll catch you later.'

I headed out of the office with Trixie at my side. The day was sunny, although the weather bureau had predicted more showers. The place I had to go to was in Selton, a tiny town northwest of Cape Carson. It wasn't far from Lily Bailey's winery.

Singing along to music on the way, I turned to Trixie who was unusually quiet. 'Is it my singing?' I asked.

She yowled.

I grumbled. 'Everyone's a critic.'

We reached Selton half an hour later. The town was so small it was hard to believe it even warranted a name. It had a service station, a café, and a general store that doubled as a post office. There were three other shops as well, but these had been long since boarded up.

I pulled in for petrol but lingered at the chocolate stand. *Oh, dear. Why do the sweets have to be so strategically placed?* Before heading off to pay, I settled on a new bar made of chocolate, marshmallows, and peanuts.

'We've got a deal going,' the pimple-faced kid behind the counter said. 'Only fifty cents for a second bar.'

Trying not to think of the calories, I bought a second one and returned to the car. Trixie gave me a look.

'I'll wear it off,' I told her. 'I just need to walk more.'

She barked.

Munching on the bar, I continued on to the address that Doreen had sent me. The place turned out to be a timber farmhouse on a side road outside of town.

Overgrown fields surrounded the place. The land was so choked with thistles and other weeds that I doubted it was even used for the agistment of cattle or sheep.

'Goodness,' I muttered, emerging from my jeep.

The place was in a terrible state. The building had once been painted white, but most of the paint had flaked off. The tin roof had holes in it. An overgrown hedge grew across the front, shielding the house from the road.

How can someone live here? Maybe Doreen's elderly.

This sometimes happened with older people when their properties became too much to handle. Their homes gradually fell into disrepair until the owner either died or was moved into an aged care facility.

It looked like Doreen was past moving on. I shoved the metal gate open, and it squealed angrily on its hinges. Knocking at the front door, I waited for an answer with Trixie at my side. She gave a worried whine.

'What is it, girl?' I asked quietly.

A faint wail came from inside the house.

'Hello?' I called.

It had sounded like a woman's voice: someone in pain.

The cry came again. I pushed the front door open. The hallway was empty apart from a rug running down its length. The kitchen at the far end looked dark and dirty. *This place is in a real state.* It was amazing it hadn't been condemned.

The cry came again, louder this time, and I stepped forward. Trixie gave another whine, and I glanced down at her.

'Someone needs our help,' I said.

She gave a frenzied bark as I continued forward—and then the floor soundlessly fell away beneath me. One second, I was walking; the next, I was in mid-air. There was carpet. The ceiling. Floor joists. I cried out, grabbed at a piece of timber as I fell, and swung on it like a monkey.

Snap!

The end of the timber joist broke, and I fell into the basement below. My feet hit the floor. I pitched forward.

Throwing out my hands, my head banged into a pile of shattered timber, and I was sent spinning across the floor. I landed hard and lay there stunned.

What on Earth...?

Dust filled the air. I coughed, trying to work out what had happened. The floor had given way. No. I looked upwards. There *was* no floor. The rug I'd stepped on was a covering for a gaping hole in the floorboards. I'd fallen about twelve feet into a basement. What had saved me was the floor joist I'd swung on like a monkey on the way down. As well as slowing my descent, it had helped to keep me upright. If I hadn't grabbed it, I would likely have been badly injured.

Luckily, Trixie hadn't fallen into the hole. She was smarter than me. Trixie sat whining at the edge. In fact, thinking about it now, I realised she'd been trying to warn me.

'I'm okay, girl,' I said. 'But I'll be even better once I work out what's going on.'

I sat up.

Uhh.

My ankle wasn't broken, but I'd twisted it badly. Plus, I'd banged my head on what was once a staircase leading down here but was now a pile of broken boards. All right, I thought. I'm down here. Where's the woman who was crying out? Was that Doreen Hollis? Has she been injured—

A chill ran through me.

Oh no.

I'd been a complete idiot.

'Hello?' I called. 'Who's there?'

I wasn't expecting Doreen Hollis to answer. If my guess was correct, there *was no Doreen Hollis*. This was a trap. At least I had my phone. I'd dropped my bag in the fall. Scrambling through my purse, I pulled it out and stared in disbelief. *There are no bars.* How is that possible? I always had a signal, and I'd driven out this way a hundred times. I tried calling the emergency triple zero number, but nothing happened.

This makes no sense.

Triple zero calls transmitted on any available mobile network in the country, regardless of your provider. I should have been able to connect.

I peered about the gloom. The floor was stone. So were the walls. This had once been someone's home, but it had long since fallen to ruin. I grabbed a scrap of timber from what used to be the staircase. It crumbled in my fingers.

'Termites,' I muttered. Those were the culprits. Once they started munching through the timber, they were a relentless army, annihilating everything in their path.

Trixie peered down at me, angling her head sideways with worry.

'I'm okay, girl,' I said. 'I'm fine.'

That wasn't entirely true. At least it didn't sound like there was anyone else in the house. They were well and truly gone. Maybe they expected the fall to kill me. If not that, with no cell phone signal, then hunger would eventually get me. I thought about the remaining chocolate bar. That could be my last meal for some time. Maybe forever.

I shook my head. No. I had to be positive. There's got to be a way out of here.

But how?

Climbing the walls was impossible. Hobbling about, I picked up first one piece of timber and then another in the vain hope that I could form a makeshift ladder. The wood cracked into pieces.

Well, that's not going to work.

I heard the distant rumble of an engine.

A car!

It could be the killer returning. Or maybe it was someone passing by. Either way, I had to risk it.

I took a deep breath. 'Hey!' I yelled. 'Hey! I'm down here. I'm down—'

The sound of the vehicle receded into the distance. I thought about how pitiful my voice must sound from outside. The distance from me to the road was about thirty feet. My voice might carry that far, but any passing vehicle was going at high speed. There was no chance they'd hear me yelling.

I folded my arms as the basement closed in around me. I was stuck down here with no way out.

27

I could see the headline now:

Mummified Corpse of Reporter Found in Basement

How did I end up in this situation? My own naivety brought me here. I was lucky the killer hadn't waited behind a door and hacked me to death with an axe. Or worse.

But who was he? I tried to put my worry aside and focus on the case. This began with the deaths at the Bailey house. Something in connection with those deaths brought Sofia Russo back to Cape Carson. She met someone at that house who murdered her. He dumped her body off the coast and discarded her belongings. Then he killed James Nelson.

Why? What did James Nelson know about Justin and Claire Bailey? Was it something from that night? Did he know who killed them? If so, why hadn't he spoken up before now?

Trixie delivered a plaintive whine.

'I'm okay, Trixie,' I said.

If worst came to worst, I could send Trixie to get help. A

car would eventually stop if they saw her running about in the middle of nowhere, but I hoped it wouldn't come to that. Trixie could also get dognapped, and I didn't want that to happen either.

My eyes settled on the beam I had briefly grabbed on the way down. It was several feet overhead. I had no chance of reaching it, but if I could lasso it...

Oh boy, I thought. *Good thing there's no one else to see this.*

I stripped down to my underwear and shoved my phone into my bra. I tied one end of my pants leg to the end of the shirt sleeve. *My girl guide training is finally coming in handy.* Then I tied a rudimentary loop with the other shirt sleeve. Now I had a basic lasso at the end of my makeshift rope. It wasn't as effective as tying sheets together, but it would have to do.

Swinging it about, I tossed the loop end upwards, trying to snag the end of the floor joist. Missed. I tried again. Missed again. I tried another half a dozen times before the lasso finally caught over the end.

Yes!

I coaxed it along the length of the exposed joist towards the wall. This way, I could use it like an abseiler climbing up or down a rockface, my feet pressed against the stone wall.

Gripping the end of the pants, I braced my feet against the wall, found some traction, and pulled myself up. I dragged myself up another foot, cursing my lack of fitness. *If I get out of this alive, I'm cutting down on jumbo double-shot caramel lattes!* Sweat ran down my face as I hoisted myself, inch by inch, up the length of the makeshift rope, my feet scrambling for purchase as I ascended.

This is horrible.

But now, I was only a few feet away from the joist. Three feet. Two feet. Then—

Grasping the joist end with one hand, then the other, I hung there exhausted for a few seconds before I pulled myself onto the beam.

Trixie whined.

I'm okay, girl.

I couldn't speak. I was breathing too hard. Sweat and dirt peppered my face and my hands were shaking. Reaching across, I dragged myself across to the floorboards.

I did it. I did it. I did it.

I lay there, breathing hard as Trixie licked my face.

'I'm all right, girl,' I said. 'I'm all right.'

My handbag and jacket were still in the basement, but that was okay. I had my phone. After untying my clothing, I put my pants and shirt back on and stumbled back to my jeep. I felt sick and dizzy from the effort of climbing. I flopped behind the wheel, breathing heavily until I could speak.

Then I rang Todd.

Half an hour later, he and Jim Turner arrived. The constable asked me questions while Todd looked around the place. He returned a few minutes later with my jacket, handbag and an electronic device in a plastic bag.

'This is what stopped you from calling,' he said. 'It's a tiny jamming device. Short-range, it's powerful enough to stop any incoming or outgoing calls. There's no sign of any weeping woman.'

'Do you know who owns the property?' I asked.

'I made some inquiries on the way here. It's a farmer who went into a nursing home a few years back. That's why the place is in such a bad state.' Todd asked Turner to take another look around while he took me to one side. 'Are you sure you're all right?'

'I'm fine,' I said, although I felt like crying. It wasn't every day that someone tried to kill me. 'Just feeling a bit battered and exhausted.'

'Then you've got to go to the hospital.'

'I'm fine. I don't need—'

'Hospital,' he said, firmly.

I *had* hit my head on the way down, so it was probably a good idea. Sometimes concussions didn't show up for hours. Or days.

'Okay,' I agreed. 'Hospital.'

The rest of my day was spent at Cape Carson hospital, where I underwent tests. At my insistence, Todd didn't ring Nan. I didn't want her to worry, especially as how I was essentially fine. He did contact Kim, though, who didn't mince words.

'Wow,' she said, open-mouthed when she saw me in the waiting room. 'You look terrible!'

'Thanks,' I said, laughing. 'I've felt better.'

My ankle was aching badly by now, but it wasn't anything that a few painkillers wouldn't fix. Kim insisted on driving me home in my car. She could retrieve hers later from the hospital.

'You know what this means?' Kim said as we zigzagged through the Cape Carson streets. 'This means you're getting close.'

I leaned back in the seat. 'I think you're right.'

'At this rate, you'll be lucky to make it through the week—'

'Yeah, thanks. Maybe I should make out my will.'

Kim nodded thoughtfully. 'Probably a good idea.'

I loved Kim, but sometimes she could be horribly blunt. Although, she was right in what she was saying. I was getting closer to the truth. The problem was that I didn't know what that was!

Reaching home, I thanked her and headed inside. Nan had been watching from the veranda.

'What happened to you?' she asked suspiciously.

'I fell over.'

'You always were a terrible liar.'

Sighing, I then told her what had happened.

'That mongrel!' she snapped. 'He's got to be stopped before someone else gets hurt.'

Or she's got to be stopped, I thought.

I was thinking about Lily Bailey. The winery wasn't that far away from where I'd been lured.

It was late in the day now, and Nan offered to make dinner. I suggested we get a pizza delivered, but she insisted on pasta and had it ready in minutes. By then, Kim had rung and turned up to join us.

'So Rosie's told you all her adventures?' Kim said to Nan.

'Only half of them,' Nan said. 'She knew the other half would turn my hair grey—and I didn't want to waste good money on hair dye!'

After dinner, Nan and I worked on the memory quilt while Kim plied us with tea and biscuits. Kim picked up a button from Nan's box of scraps and examined it.

'What's this, Nan?' she asked.

Nan eyed the button and chuckled. 'That's from Frank's old ski jacket,' she said. 'We used to go skiing at Mount Buller. Well,' she amended, 'we were *on* skis. We spent as much time sliding on our butts as we did skiing.' Taking the button from Kim, she thoughtfully attached it to the quilt. 'Time goes quick, girls. Make the most of it. Sometimes, all you have left in the end are your memories and buttons. That's all: memories and buttons.'

28

I was determined to move ahead in this investigation, and I could think of only one way of doing that: I had to speak to Wayne Price. John Bailey had said Wayne was infatuated with his mother, and I needed to discover if that were true.

Limping down to Sandy's Diner early the following day, I arrived to find Sandy wiping down the counter.

'What happened to you?' she asked.

'Another night of Russian folk dancing.'

'That'll get you every time.'

'Mind if I chat to Wayne?'

'Sure.'

I settled in near the window and looked out at the sea. Sandy made me a coffee, and I took grateful sips, feeling more alert with every passing second. *Whoever invented caffeine deserves a medal.* Looking out at the beach, I saw a familiar figure marching resolutely down the path.

That's Blossom, I thought.

George appeared from behind, raced up, and grabbed her arm. Turning, she shook him off. I couldn't read lips, but I could read their body language. It was an argument. They stood and spoke for another minute before they continued down the footpath.

Looks like they're not happy.

I tried to feel pleased, but I couldn't. What George and Blossom had done was awful. No denying that. But I didn't like to see anyone in pain. Not even them.

Sandy sidled over. 'Wayne will just be a minute,' she said. 'He's got a big order of pancakes out there. But I wanted to give you some good news. I've been in contact with the South Coast car club, and they're interested in being part of the festival.'

Festival?

Oh. The rock and roll festival. 'Wow,' I said. 'That's great.'

'And we're talking about raising money for a good cause.'

'Who were you thinking of?'

'The local hospital.'

'That's a great choice,' I said. 'I did a story a while back about the hospital. Their facilities need a serious upgrade.'

'We might be able to get them some new equipment,' Sandy said. 'Oh, here's Wayne.'

The older man sidled over and sat down as Sandy headed back to the counter.

'Sandy said you wanted to talk about something,' Wayne said.

I had to be delicate about this. 'I've been following up on the story about the Bailey house,' I said. 'Been talking to a lot of people.' He nodded. 'There were obviously a lot of issues between Justin and Claire.'

'They used to fight like cats and dogs.'

'I've been told that Justin had a female friend he was seeing on the side.'

Wayne sighed. 'I wondered if you'd find out about that,' he said. 'That was Gabriel. She was Justin's *special* friend.'

'And she used to visit the house?'

'She did. Sometimes it was even when Claire was home. She'd come in through the back garden, and he'd let her in through the secret stairs. Neither Sofia nor I dared say anything about it. We were only the hired help. It wasn't our business to interfere, and we would have been sacked if we had.'

'I see.' I eyed Wayne carefully. 'I was told that Claire had an admirer of her own. Someone closer to home.'

His gaze settled on me, and a wry smile crossed his face. 'You asking if I had a thing for Claire? Sure I did. Just about every man fell instantly in love with her.' He stopped. 'Oh, I see. Now you're wondering if I had anything to do with Justin and Claire's deaths.'

I said nothing.

'I did argue with Justin the day of the murders,' Wayne continued. 'He was behind on my pay again, and I was sick of it. But I would never have harmed him. And Claire could have walked out at any time, and she didn't. She stayed with Justin, and it cost Claire her life.'

'So you loved Claire?'

He shrugged. 'I suppose,' he said. 'And would I have run away with Claire? Sure. But that would never happen. We were different people. She was married and had kids. It was one of those things that could never be.'

A bell chimed in the kitchen.

'They're playing my song,' he said. 'I'd better get moving.'

I thanked him for his time, and he left.

Sipping on my coffee, I wondered how all this fit together. Twenty years ago, it seemed everyone had issues with Justin and Claire Bailey.

Justin owed Wayne money. He owed James Nelson money too. Giuseppe's business dealings with Justin had soured. And Justin and Gabriel were having an affair. There could have been a lover's spat between them that spiralled out of control. Then, of course, Wayne was secretly in love with Claire. Wayne was the first person into the room. He *could* have lied about the door being locked.

Both the Bailey children were beneficiaries of their parent's will. That made for motive to kill them. John Bailey's girlfriend had died not long before his parents. The stress of that *could* have driven him over the edge. Or Lily *could* have killed them. By all accounts, she had a terrible temper. She had, after all, broken the nose of another girl at school.

And then there was Sofia Russo. How did she fit into all this? She obviously contacted someone using a burner phone, and agreed to meet them at the Bailey house. What did she know that got her murdered? And why did she take so long to share it?

Something was wrong with all this. All the pieces were there, but a crucial part of the puzzle hadn't slotted into place.

After paying at the counter, I left and took a stroll down to the beach, where I took out my phone and rang Todd.

'How are you doing?' he asked.

'Fine,' I said, although I felt like a wreck. 'I wanted to ask if you'd been back to the Bailey house.'

He told me he and Jim Turner had returned to conduct a second search. They'd discovered nothing unusual. 'We didn't find any evidence,' Todd said. 'Although it was probably the place where Sofia Russo was murdered. I'm inclined to think that your friend Edna Crayborne did spot the murder taking place.'

'Have you learnt anything about James Nelson's murder?'

Todd sighed. 'There's no evidence it *was* a murder,' he said. 'The man fell off the cliff.'

'He was pushed!'

'Maybe. But there's no evidence, and we need evidence to pursue a crime.'

Anger welled up inside me. 'You know who you sound like?' I said. 'Your predecessor—Sergeant Wilson.'

'Peter Wilson was a dedicated member of the police force.'

'He was a blowhard!' I snapped. 'Do you know how many defect notices he issued to my car? Three!'

Todd's voice was cold. 'Have you ever thought that maybe you deserved it?' he asked. 'Your jeep *is* a little worse for wear.'

My anger flared. 'I didn't ask for your opinion about my car,' I said. 'When I want it, I'll let you know.'

'Fine.'

Something horribly final in the way he said *fine* made me realise I'd taken things too far.

'All right,' I said. 'Then I'll go.'

'That's probably for the best.'

My chest was quaking as I hung up, and my vision blurred as tears filled my eyes. I crossed to a nearby bench and sat down. A jogger ran past as I wiped away a tear. The conversation kept replaying in my mind. His words. My words.

Trixie whined as she put her head on my knee.

'Oh, Trixie,' I said. 'I've really made a mess of things.'

29

It took me another half an hour to properly compose myself, so I could head into the office. Harry glanced up from his desk and took one look at me.

'Go home,' he said.

'But—'

'That's an order.'

I wanted to argue, but that would have been pointless.

Harry was right. My body was a wreck, and my brain felt like it had been put through a blender. Driving home, I pulled into the driveway and burst into tears again.

Fortunately, Nan was out. I remembered her saying she was going on a drive with Dave. That was for the best. I was in no mood to talk to anyone about how I felt. As I climbed into bed, Trixie lay on the floor beside me. I curled into a ball and had another good cry.

I wasn't sure why I felt so terrible. Maybe it was all my aches and pains. Or it may have been because I'd poured weed killer over my budding romance with a guy who I'd come to like. I didn't know if Todd Parker was *the one*, but at least he was one-*ish*.

When I awoke, I found myself staring directly into Trixie's face. She was on the bed beside me, her face in mine. Lifting her head, she gave a small whine. I glanced at my bedside clock. *3.00pm*. The whole day had passed. I really must have been in a bad state. Climbing out of bed, I found Nan in the living room, working on the quilt.

'You're alive!' she declared.

'Only just.' I went to the kitchen, tossed some cereal into a bowl, and made a cup of tea. 'I'll be in the backyard if you need me.'

I settled onto an outdoor chair, ate my cereal, and sipped my tea. Closing my eyes, I listened as an eastern rosella in a tree called to its mate. The sound was answered by a reply. Opening my eyes, I spotted a flash of red and green as one bird joined another, and they disappeared from sight.

It looked like they were having more luck than me.

That's it, I thought. *I'm giving up on relationships.*

Maybe I'd become a nun.

No. That was silly.

I was a journalist and a reasonably good one. An idea had been teasing at the edge of my thoughts since I'd awoken, and now it came to the foreground. This mystery started twenty years ago with the deaths of Justin and Claire Bailey. If there were an answer to be found, it would be at the old Bailey house.

After finishing my tea, I traipsed inside with Trixie at my side and grabbed my handbag.

'Where are you going?' Nan asked, glancing up from the quilt.

'I've got work to do.'

'Is it that Bailey house?'

'Where else? I'm going there to sort this thing out once and for all.'

It would have been nice to have Kim with me, but she was working. I headed for the car. The sky had come over cloudy during the day, and it was raining by the time I arrived at the house. Soon I was closing the front door behind me.

The house silently greeted me as I stood there, listening to the rain falling outside. Lightning flashed across the darkened floor.

Despite only being here a few times, I felt like I'd returned to a place I knew well. This is where my journey began. This was where it would finish.

'Hello, old friend,' I murmured. 'I'm back.'

The silent house said nothing, but Trixie whined, and I ruffled her neck. 'It's okay, girl,' I said. 'We're just taking a look around.'

I headed down to the basement. The underground room had the same closed-in feeling as before: as if I were buried alive. Grey light seeped in through the casement window. The corners of the room were clad in darkness. It was easy to believe that ghosts dwelt there. A rustling came from the gloom, and my heart almost exploded in my chest. Then a mouse scurried across the floor and disappeared into a hole in the wall.

Returning upstairs, I examined the kitchen, living room, and bathroom before heading to the first floor to check out the bedrooms, study, and office. If I were expecting another dead body, I was sorely disappointed. The house was empty and quiet.

Soon I was traipsing up the final staircase to the attic. As I pushed the door open, lightning flashed across the interior, and the house vibrated as distant thunder crawled across the sky.

This is it, I thought. *The start. The finish.*

I crossed to the far end, activated the secret door, and it clicked open. Using my phone to light the way, I followed the stairs down to the exit at the other end. Opening the door, I peered out into the pouring rain. Thunder rumbled across the sky again, and Trixie whined at my side.

'It's okay, girl,' I said. 'It's nothing.'

We headed back up the stairs to the attic, and I clicked the door shut behind me. I remembered the crime scene photos that Ellie had shown me back at the office. Some had been taken at almost the same angle as pictures from the lifestyle photoshoot. I brought both pictures up on my phone.

The room was different now. The cabinets were empty. The furniture and sound system were gone. And, of course, the two pictures on my phone were different too. The first showed Justin and Claire Bailey proudly showing off the attic. Justin stood behind the tiny bar. Claire lay on the vintage chaise lounge. Spencer sat in his cage.

The second photo was apparently innocent, but it had been taken when both Justin and Claire were dead. The room appeared unchanged. Furniture and furnishings were in the same position. The cabinets still stuffed with curios. Costumes hung in place. Theatre mannequins crowded the room.

And yet...

The same nagging feeling stirred my gut. Something was wrong. Something was different. What was it?

I strode up and down the length of the attic. There were so many mysteries connected with this case. But what was the most baffling part of this mystery? At first, I thought it was the mystery of the three bullets, although that could be explained; the witnesses might have been wrong. It wasn't the death of Sofia Russo either. She knew something about Justin and Claire's deaths. No. There was an even bigger question.

Why was James Nelson killed?

He was an architect. And he knew about the secret passage because he helped design it. Did the builders know about the secret passage? It was just another set of stairs without the secret doors at the top and bottom. Lily Bailey had said her father helped with construction. What did she say?

Some of the building work right at the end was completed by him.

My eyes scanned the attic.

This place still had more secrets to reveal.

I crossed to the bar and felt around the edges. Then I moved to the windows and grabbed and rattled the sills. Down on my hands and knees, I felt along each edge of the skirting boards. Most of the cornice was out of reach, but I grabbed and shook every piece I could. Moving to the display cabinets, I ran my hands around the outside edges of the timber carpentry before searching the interior.

At the end of a long hour, I had discovered nothing. I was no wiser than I'd been at the start of my search.

My gaze moved about the room.

What am I not seeing?

What was so obvious, so innocuous, that I had not noticed it? I forced myself to take in every last detail. The door handle. The light fittings. The power switches. The—

And then I saw it.

30

A single power switch was situated on the skirting board at the far end of the room. All the other switches were doubles.

Why is that a single switch?

I crossed to it, quickly dropped to one knee, and grabbed the switch housing. It seemed solid. I flicked the switch. Nothing was plugged in, and there was no power anyway, so I had no idea if it was operational.

Years ago, I had seen a dummy power switch that someone had installed in their home to hide precious jewellery. I couldn't remember how it opened. Maybe it slid or maybe pushing—

Click!

I slowly turned to see the section of the wall beside the secret passage disengage. My heart pounding, I crossed to the wall, gripped it, and pulled hard. Shining my torch into the space beyond, I saw a narrow, winding staircase leading downwards.

Trixie tilted her head quizzically.

'That's right, Trixie,' I said. 'It's a second secret passage. A *real* secret passage.' I peered down the dark stairs. 'It's clever when you think about it. What's the best way to hide a secret? *Tell people.* Let them think they know it, and they don't stop to wonder if you have another. That's what Justin Bailey did. He built two secret passages and told everyone about one of them. It's classic misdirection.'

Trixie whined as she followed me down the stairs. An idea was forming in the back of my mind. I thought I knew where this was leading. *Now to see if I'm right.* The passageway was tiny in spots. It looked like James Nelson's original plans were for the first passage to be twice as wide. Justin had obviously ordered him to split it in two.

Mostly it followed the other passage, but as it reached the ground floor, it veered into another direction.

Finally, I arrived at a blank wall. After pushing on it for several seconds, I spotted a tiny button at the top. I pressed on it and was rewarded with another faint *click*. The wall slowly swung open to reveal another gloomy space.

The basement.

Lightning flashed, pouring grey light through the casement window. I stepped into the cold underground room. This was where I thought I'd end up. I wasn't afraid, though. The gloomy basement with its darkened corners didn't scare me. All the pieces of the puzzle were coming together. All I needed was—

And that's when it hit me. It was as if a light had exploded in my mind. I scrolled through the photos on my phone: the first one with Justin and Claire and the later one after their deaths. Now, finally, I saw what was different. No wonder it had been so hard to notice. It wasn't what was there. It was what was *missing*.

Lightning flashed again. Blinking, I thought my eyes were playing tricks on me as a section of darkness disengaged from the gloom.

It rushed towards me. Before I could react, something reached out and slammed into my head. The phone fell from my hand, and everything went black. I floated in a silent deep ocean.

I seemed to drift in that quiet water forever. Then I heard the ocean crashing against the shoreline. Waves beating against the rocks.

No. Not waves. An engine.

Is it a boat?

I slowly returned to consciousness. There was no ocean. No boat. What followed was a far more horrible realisation. *I've been buried alive.* But coffins were small and silent, and I was sprawled across a hard, uneven surface. I was wrapped in something. A hard object pressed uncomfortably into my back, and everything was swaying from side to side.

The answer came out of nowhere.

I'm in the boot of someone's car.

The orange and red glare from the taillights gave the interior a strange illumination, as if I were inside the Haunted House at the fairground. I could just make out what appeared to be a lump of rug in the gloom to my left. The killer must have wrapped me in it to transport me to his waiting car. It was still wrapped around me, but the motion of the car had worked me loose. Bigger issues faced me. My hands were secured behind my back. A gag filled my mouth.

It was terrible—but nothing compared to the pain in my head. I'd been hit with something hard. Maybe an iron bar. I was lucky to be alive. Maybe the killer even thought I was dead or would die on the way to where he intended to dump my body. Soon, maybe in a matter of minutes, I'd be tossed into some unmarked grave, and he'd continue on with his life.

He's thought of everything.

Except he didn't know *me*. I may not have been Lois Lane, but I was me, and that was enough. The killer hadn't reckoned on my experience as a journalist. He didn't know that I'd interviewed an escape artist soon after I first moved to Cape Carson. Daring 'Donnie' Dazzler had told me that one way to escape from the boot of a car was to kick out the taillights. With any luck, you could stick a hand or foot out to alert a passing driver.

I was still half-tangled in the rug, but one foot was near the left-hand taillight. Somehow, I'd lost my shoes, but my bare feet would be enough. I kicked hard at the plastic housing. Once. Twice. Three times. Nothing happened. I continued kicking at the plastic. I heard the vehicle slow down.

Has he heard me?

Kicking more frantically, I realised the killer had changed direction. The sound of the engine was different. He was heading up a hill. The ground was rougher too. We were driving over an unsealed road. A private property or bushland.

Summoning my strength, I kicked hard at the plastic, and it shattered. Cold air flooded the boot, and I inched downwards. Sticking my foot through the gap, I waved my toes desperately.

Please. Let there be someone out there.

Help me! Please!

The engine changed again. The car was slowing. My heart lurched. *Is this it? Is this where he's dumping my body?* Then the blare of a vehicle horn rent the air. The car I was in slowed down. Braked hard. Something smashed into the side of the killer's car.

I was momentarily airborne. My face and upper body hit the roof, and I landed again, dazed. People were yelling. There was a siren. Although my body was a bundle of pain, I knew my whole situation had changed in an instant.

Help is here! I'm going to be all right!

The sound of voices drew nearer as I struggled the gag from my mouth. I screamed. Hands raked the boot, it popped open, and I looked up to see faces I never expected to see again: Nan, Amanda, Kim, and Todd. Then they were grabbing at me and gently easing me from the cramped interior.

I had no idea how everyone had come to be here, but those answers could come later. I gazed around. It was early evening, and we were on a remote bush property. There was a police car. And there was my jeep, the front smashed in. It looked like it had been used to ram the killer's vehicle.

Trixie was barking wildly. Someone released my hands, and I gingerly rubbed my wrists. I'd been secured with cable ties. Everyone was talking at once. I couldn't answer them, though, because my gaze was fixed on the driver that Constable Turner was holding on the ground. The killer's face was alternating between two extremes as complete madness took its toll. He was both laughing and crying, almost as if he were wearing the masks from the theatre, the faces of Melpomene and Thalia.

His eyes met mine for one brief moment. 'I had to do it!' John Bailey shrieked. 'I had to!'

Then the killer was bundled into a waiting police car.

Nan gently touched my arm. 'Rosie,' she said. 'What's all this about?'

I turned to her and the others. My throat was hoarse, but I could still speak. 'It's about a murder,' I said. 'And how John

Bailey tried to cover it up by committing two other murders.'

I rubbed my throat.

'You can tell us later,' Amanda said.

'We need to get you to a hospital,' Kim said.

'Sure,' I replied. 'But can we stop by Sandy's Diner on the way? I need a caramel latte—and it better be jumbo-sized.'

31

'This was like some twisted version of Romeo and Juliet,' I said. 'But nobody realised it.'

I was sitting up in bed at the Cape Carson Public Hospital. Surrounding me in the room were Nan and Amanda and Todd and Kim. Despite being told that dogs weren't allowed in the hospital, the staff had turned a blind eye to Trixie. She was curled up on the bed beside me.

My head still hurt. The doctors had given me every kind of scan imaginable and hadn't found a fracture. I was lucky. Despite my ordeal, I hadn't suffered a single broken bone, although I had bruises from head to toe. Drugs were keeping the pain at bay, though it would take days for me to heal completely.

'I've taken a look at those original crime scene photos,' Todd said. 'You're right, Rosie. The officers at the time missed an important clue. It was unforgivable.'

Everyone looked confused.

'What do you mean?' Nan asked.

'The investigating officers found needles near Justin and Claire's bodies,' Todd continued. 'If they'd been checked, they would have found what they contained.'

'Illegal drugs?' Amanda guessed.

'No,' Todd answered, pausing. '*Adrenalin.*'

This was greeted with shocked silence.

'*Adrenalin*?' Kim finally said. 'What was it for?'

'I'll explain,' I said. 'It started at high school when John Bailey was dating a girl named Erin Fowler. Mina at the library described her to me. It sounds like Erin was nice. Too nice for a creature like John.' I glanced over at Todd. 'Let me know if I'm wrong about any of this.'

'I will.' Todd smiled grimly. 'But you're probably right.'

'My guess is that she broke up with him,' I said. 'It would have been no big deal. Just like any other teenage breakup. A few tears. Some hormonal anguish. No lasting damage. But not for John Bailey. No, not him. He came from money, and power, and privilege. I can only imagine how his mind works, but it was probably an affront to his ego.

'How dare that insignificant girl dump him? She was nothing, and he was the great John Bailey! It must have been a crushing blow for him. So she had to be punished. Erin had to pay for what she'd done. Of course, John knew Erin's weakness. She had a severe peanut allergy. It was so bad that Erin would suffer anaphylaxis, causing her mouth and throat to swell up, and she could stop breathing. It could even kill her.

'One day, about a week after they broke up, Erin accidentally bit into a sandwich that belonged to someone else. That was serious, but Erin should have been fine because she carried her medication everywhere. Adrenaline counters the effects of anaphylaxis by causing the blood vessels to shrink and airways to open up.

'Except, when she searched for it, the medication that could have saved her life was missing. Somehow, it was gone from her bag, and that tiny mistake—if it were a mistake—was fatal, and she died.'

Amanda was staring at me. '*If* it were a mistake?'

Todd cut in. 'No one was ever able to work out how the sandwiches got switched,' he said. 'Or how her medication disappeared.'

'My guess,' I continued, 'is that John purposely swapped the sandwiches and stole her medication. It couldn't have been an accident. Many people who suffer from those types of allergies don't just carry one injector.' I swallowed hard. 'They take two, and yet—somehow—both of Erin's were gone.' I let this sink in. 'John Bailey murdered her.'

Nan gasped. 'How horrible.'

'At the time, no one suspected that her ex-boyfriend would have done such a thing,' I said. 'After all, they were teenagers, and teenage relationships break up all the time. Everyone put it down to a tragic accident. Somehow, the sandwiches got switched. Somehow, she misplaced her medication. It looked like an accident,' I said. 'Except, it wasn't.'

I allowed this to settle in. Everyone looked shocked. Everyone except for Todd, who was nodding thoughtfully.

'He would have gotten away with it too,' I said. 'Except he neglected to get rid of the syringes. My guess is that one of John's parents, probably Claire, found them and confronted him. Wayne Price said there were needles near their bodies. The police noted it too. But no one thought anything of it because it was an open and shut case. The room was locked from the inside. Justin and Claire had fought, and he had shot his wife before turning the gun on himself. End of story.'

I rubbed my throat. 'John's parents were arguing that day,' I said. 'That wasn't unusual, but my guess is they were arguing about John. They were probably talking about going to the police—and that's where they underestimated their son. They didn't think it through. You see, John had already committed one murder. That was enough to land him in jail for years. His life would be ruined, and his reputation destroyed. They didn't realise how desperate John would be to cover up his crime.'

'But how did he kill them?' Kim asked. 'John Bailey was downstairs when it happened. Both Sofia and Wayne were with him in the kitchen.'

'The Baileys had a full house the night they were killed,' I said. 'Justin and Claire were in the attic. Lily was in her room. Giuseppe Costa was in the office, and James Nelson was in the library. As you say, John was with the staff in the kitchen when the shots were heard. He seemed to have the perfect alibi.'

I took a long breath. This would take some explaining.

'After his parents discovered that he'd murdered Erin, John knew he had to work quickly. He had to act fast, or his whole life would fall apart. John must have already known about the second secret passage. I suspect he'd discovered it by accident one day.'

Todd nodded. 'That's true,' he said. 'He told us he found it while hooking up some speakers.'

'John already had everything ready before he went up the second secret stairs to the attic. His parents would have been completely taken by surprise. One moment they were yelling at each other. The next, part of the wall slid aside, and John emerged.

'He was fast. You've probably seen movies where assassins use a makeshift silencer to dull the sound of gunshots. John had probably removed the gun from the cabinet earlier. Now, he shot his father by wrapping a cushion around the weapon to muffle the sound of the gunshot. If Claire screamed, no one would have noticed. She and Justin had been yelling at each other for hours. One more scream meant nothing.

'Anyway, within seconds, she was dead as well. There was probably some mess. The cushion John used was filled with feathers. People saw the feathers on the floor and assumed they were from Spencer, the bird. Some were, but I'd be willing to bet good money that a lot were from the cushion when it was used to silence the gunshots.'

'So how many shots were there?' Kim asked.

'Two,' I said.

'But some people said they heard three shots.'

'Ah, yes,' I said. 'That mysterious third shot.'

'So were there two shots or three?' Nan asked.

'The gun was only fired two times—but there were three gunshots.'

Amanda frowned. 'Three?' she said. 'But how—'

Despite my aching head, I gave a bitter laugh. 'The murders happened *earlier* than everyone realised. John Bailey loved sound recording, so he'd probably previously recorded his parents arguing, maybe as one of his experiments. John also had a special effects collection that included gunshots.

'That afternoon, he quickly created a composite recording of his parents arguing, followed by gunfire. After murdering his parents, he put a memory card into the sound system and hit play. This was what everyone heard: the recorded sound of the Baileys' arguing and then the gunshots.

'It went completely to plan—except John made a mistake. An absolute doozy. Remember, all this was done on the fly. It would have been easy to make a mistake.

'And he did. When he added the sound of the gunfire to the recording, he accidentally added *three* shots. He must have been horrified when he realised what he'd done. It was a huge blunder, but there was nothing he could do about it.'

'So what everyone heard was a recording?' Nan said.

I nodded. 'After John hit play, he raced down the secret staircase and came up from the basement to join Sofia and Wayne in the kitchen. They gave him the perfect alibi for when the shots finally rang out. John then followed the others to the attic, all the while pretending to be the concerned son. Later he swore he heard only two shots. He had to convince people that there'd only *been* two shots. Of course, the memory card was in the sound system, but no one looked twice at it. Why would they? It was obvious what had happened. A murder-suicide.

'The bigger mistake was leaving the syringes. John should have taken them away, but, you see, he was in a rush. And things worked out to his benefit, anyway. People saw these odd-looking needles beside the Baileys' bodies and thought nothing of it.

'Later, after the bodies were removed, John returned to the attic and removed the memory card. Nothing remained to show that he'd gotten away with murder.'

Nan frowned. 'Until this Sofia Russo woman turned up.'

I nodded. 'John's been creating experimental music for years,' I said. 'I imagine that's when everything began to fall apart. Sofia probably downloaded one and realised that what she and the others heard on the night could have been a recording. She may not have known about Erin's death, although she probably did.'

Todd intervened. 'I think she did,' he said. 'We combed the browsing history on Sofia's computer. There were searches on there about peanut allergies and medication.'

'Okay,' I said. 'So it must have all clicked. And I'm assuming Sofia was down on her luck?'

'She was,' Todd confirmed. 'Sofia was trying to blackmail John Bailey.'

'She knew that John had some serious money,' I said. 'And she saw a way of getting some of it for herself. Sofia's fatal mistake was agreeing to meet him at the house. I'm sure John went there intending to kill her. It was just bad luck that Sofia reached out as he was strangling her, and she dragged the blind down. That's when Edna Crayborne saw her.'

I fixed my gaze on Todd. 'John cleaned the room where he killed Sofia, and moved her body to the second secret staircase,' I said. 'The police turned up at the house. They searched everywhere—even the secret passage that everyone knew about—but didn't find a body. When it was dark, John returned and carried the body out the back gate to his car. Then he dumped Sofia off a headland, hoping she'd never be found.

'John had to make certain she wasn't identified. He went to the hotel, not knowing that Kim and I were already there. We followed him, but he gave us the slip. That's when we ended up in the ditch, and Todd came to our rescue.'

Todd frowned. 'You didn't mention the hotel before.'

'Must have slipped my mind,' I said hastily. Best to gloss over that for the moment. 'John might have gotten away with Sofia remaining an unidentified person, but we got lucky when I found Sofia's possessions in the national park.'

'So how did James Nelson get involved in this?' Kim asked.

I sighed. 'That was partly my fault,' I said. 'I mentioned to John that I was visiting James Nelson. John panicked. Only three people knew about the second secret passage: John, his father, and James Nelson. Probably Justin Bailey had sworn Nelson to secrecy years before as part of their contract. Since then, the subject of the second secret passage had never come up, probably because there'd been no suspicions around Claire and Justin's deaths. If I mentioned that serious questions were now being raised, James Nelson might finally mention the second secret passage.' I was thoughtful. 'I imagine John visited the architect unannounced. The poor man didn't suspect a thing. They probably went for a stroll around the property.

When they were close to the edge, John Bailey pushed him over.'

'And what about the broken window at our place?' Nan asked.

Todd spoke up. 'John Bailey's admitted to breaking your window in an attempt to scare Rosie off.'

'We don't scare easy,' Nan snorted and turned to me. 'So you went back to the Bailey place and searched it again. Did you already know about the second secret passage?'

'No,' I confessed. 'I didn't know what I was searching for. Not until it was almost too late. I put everything together, and that's when John attacked me.'

'How do you know your theory about the cushions is right?' Amanda asked.

'Because of the photos,' I said. 'There was a photoshoot of the Baileys in the Gazette a week before the murders happened. It showed the attic in great detail. The paper also had access to some of the crime photos taken immediately after the murders. The photos are identical except for one thing.'

Kim gasped.

I laughed. 'Yep,' I said. 'Kim's got it. A cushion is missing in the crime scene photos. That got me wondering what could have happened to it. One thing led to another, and all the pieces fell into place.' I stopped. 'It's strange that so much of this case hinges on sound and what people heard—or thought they heard.'

'What about the painting at the house?' Nan asked. 'The one that was upside down? And the screams?'

Todd answered. 'John Bailey's told us he used to visit the house quite regularly. He used recordings of screams and gunshots to keep the locals away. John happened to be there at the same time as Rosie and Kim. He used the second passage to manoeuvre around the house to move the painting, and play the recording that created the sounds.'

'He's a wily character,' Nan commented.

'He's insane,' Todd said. 'But also quite intelligent. He set the trap at that abandoned house in Selton, thinking the fall would kill Rosie. If it didn't, she'd starve to death, anyway. He's admitted to building the jamming device that stopped her from making calls. Oh, and he had a recording of a weeping woman to lure her inside.'

'Both smart and crazy,' I said, thoughtfully. I was feeling tired, but there were a few things I needed to know. 'Now it's your turn. How did you find me? What made you follow John Bailey?'

'It was Trixie,' Nan said promptly. 'She came racing home. John Bailey must have waited till after sunset to move you. It took Trixie that long to get back to our place. I immediately knew that something was wrong. Dave had gone out for a walk—'

'And Tom was at work,' Amanda said. 'So we borrowed Dave's car and drove to the house.'

'Nan rang me on the way,' Kim said. 'I happened to be on a run and turned up just as John Bailey was driving off.'

'We weren't sure what to do,' Nan continued. 'But then Trixie kept barking crazily at his car. We knew we had to follow, and doing that in Dave's car would have been too obvious....'

Kim produced a set of keys. 'You remember when you lent me your car last year?' she said. 'When I put my car in for repairs?'

'That's right,' I said, staring at the keys. I never did get that spare set back. 'So you followed in my car?'

'And that's when I come into the story,' Todd said. 'Nan rang me, and I joined the chase.'

Amanda continued. 'John Bailey had just turned onto that property when we saw the taillight break away and a foot poke out.'

'I knew it was your foot,' Nan said. 'I'd recognise that big foot anywhere.'

'Thanks,' I said. 'I think.'

'Nan yelled out to stop his car,' Kim said, grinning. 'And I thought to myself, *Hang on, I can ram him off the road! It'll be great!*'

Everyone stared at her.

'Well,' Kim amended. 'You know what I mean.'

I thought back to when the boot had opened, and I'd peered up at their assembled faces. I'd seen some beautiful sights in my life, but that was one I'd never forget. It was almost worth getting my car damaged—and at least it could be fixed. Dave had said he knew a panel beater who could repair the damage.

At that moment, the door to my room eased open. Harry Blackshore stuck his head through. 'Well,' he said. 'Nice to see she's alive.'

Nan chuckled. 'And has she got a story to tell!'

'Really? Then I'm the man to hear it. We're holding the front page, and Rosie will probably be the lead story. I can see it now: *Intrepid Reporter Solves Twenty Year Mystery.*'

Although I rolled my eyes, I couldn't help but feel a little pleased. The headline had a Lois Lane ring to it. 'Aren't we supposed to *report* the news?' I said. 'Not *be* it?'

'True,' Harry agreed. 'But there are exceptions to every rule.' Taking out his notebook, he settled on the edge of the bed. 'Now tell me what happened—and don't leave out anything!'

32

The walk I took to Cut Rock a few days later was one of the most pleasant of my life. That's one thing about almost dying. It gives you a fresh appreciation for living. After two days in the hospital, I was allowed home, and on the third went for my first long walk. Trixie happily trotted beside me as I followed the track through the bush. It was late in the day, and the sun was close to setting, but I didn't mind. Soon the wind was pushing against my face as I ascended the final incline to the lookout and gazed over the great heaving waters of the Southern Ocean.

'Wow,' I said and looked down at Trixie. I was grinning stupidly. I couldn't stop myself, and I didn't care. 'Wow.'

A lot had happened in the last few days. A special edition of The Cape Carson Gazette had gone to print, and Harry had been as good as his word: I'd made the front page. The story wasn't entirely about me, but a chunk of it was as it revealed the truth of the Bailey murders. Undoubtedly, there'd be an update in the next edition: John Bailey would go to trial for his crimes and likely spend a long time in jail.

I'd rung Lily Bailey, but she'd refused to speak to me. I felt for her. As well as trying to run her business, she now had to deal with the revelations about her brother. At least she finally knew the truth. Her father hadn't killed her mother. They had both been victims. Maybe that would give her some comfort.

I closed my eyes. There was something joyous in simple things like standing on the coast and feeling the wind on my face. I had a family, a dog, a career, and a home. The only thing I didn't have was a partner. I was still searching for Mister *Right*, and—truth be told—even Mister *Reasonably Okay* would be acceptable.

The sound of a friendly bark came from the road, and I glanced back to see Rocko with Todd close behind. The day was fresh but sunny, and he'd chosen to show off his muscled physique.

I grinned. 'Todd, is it my imagination, or have you lost some muscle definition?'

'It's your imagination,' Todd said, although he smiled as he said it. 'To be honest, I'm cutting back on my training. It's important to be fit, but it's easy to take things too far.'

'Really?' I said. 'What brought that on?'

He stroked his chin. 'It's funny how we're reflections of our parents,' he said. 'Although I'm not much like my dad, I can still hear his voice in my head telling me to train and practice and be stronger. He was always telling me I had to be tough. I had to be powerful. I wouldn't have an acting career if I didn't train.' Todd shook his head. 'He always said I had to be a man.'

'I have no idea what that means,' I said. 'What's *being a man*?'

'It's certainly not what my father thought it was.'

'Is it because of him that you hadn't done anything about your eyesight?'

'Dad always said only weak people went to doctors.' He looked down. 'It sounds stupid even saying it. Anyway, I've been to a specialist. He'll operate on my eyes one at a time.'

'When's the first operation?'

'Next Friday.'

'That's great news! Then we've got to celebrate.'

He laughed. 'Okay,' he said. 'It's a date.'

'You can come to our place and sample my cooking,' I said. 'Despite Nan saying it's barely edible, my ex-husband survived on it for years.'

Smiling, he said we'd talk during the week. I waved him goodbye as he and Rocko trotted off. Watching until he was a tiny dot in the distance, I finally turned to Trixie and smiled.

'What do you think about all that?'

Trixie gave a happy bark.

Feeling like I was walking on air, I headed back home and arrived to find Nan in an extraordinarily good mood. The memory quilt had taken pride of place on our wall. It was the first thing people would see when they walked in the front door. Pop's shirts, pants, handkerchiefs, overalls, and dozens of other fragments of clothing blended in a cohesive whole to form a single piece of art.

'That's beautiful,' I said, hugging Nan. 'You're a clever woman.'

Nan's eyes misted over. 'I miss him,' she said. 'There's not a day goes by that I don't think of him.'

'I know. I love you, Nan.'

She gave me a tight squeeze. 'I love you too, Rosie.'

I glanced at my watch. It was almost dark, but I already felt like another excursion. Heading out the door with Trixie at my side, I stood on the street with no idea where to go.

Ah-ha, I thought. *I know.*

I walked through town. The horizon was painted mustard yellow by the time I reached the old Bailey house. Edna Crayborne was taking her dog, Mister Smith, for a walk. She crossed the road to chat.

'Nice to see you're still kicking,' Edna said. 'I read about all your adventures. Who would have thought that John Bailey was so crazy?'

'Sometimes, you can't tell.'

'Well, you did a good thing.' Her eyes angled up to the Bailey place, and she didn't speak for a moment. 'That house is different now.'

'Different?' I stared up at the gothic structure. 'How do you mean?'

Edna shook her head. 'It's hard to say,' she said. 'It just seems like an old house now. Someone could even move in.'

I peered up at it. 'That would be nice.'

Wishing me goodnight, Edna headed off with Mister Smith, and they disappeared into her home. I gazed up at the Bailey place. *Someone could move in there.* A family could fill it with fun and laughter and everything that makes up a life. My eyes shifted to the attic window.

I frowned.

What the—?

There were two shapes at the window. Two shadowy forms. One was larger. A man. The other had to be a woman. It couldn't be...

My phone rang.

I blinked—and they were gone.

Absently dragging my phone out, I hit the answer button. 'Hey, Rosie,' Harry's voice came bellowing down the line. 'You coming to work tomorrow?'

I drew my eyes away from the house.

'Sure,' I said. 'What's up?'

'There's a woman who's spent nine years painting her own version of the Mona Lisa.'

'You're kidding.'

'You think that's strange? Someone stole it.'

'What?' I scribbled down the woman's address. 'I'll go and see her now.'

'Great. And get plenty of pictures.'

I promised I would and hung up. 'Let's go, girl,' I said to Trixie. 'We've got a story to cover.'

But the adventure doesn't end here!

Catch Rosie's next mystery in:

Rings, Rocks and Murder!

ABOUT THE AUTHOR

Darrell Pitt is a prolific author, with more than two dozen novels in print. Writing for both young and old alike, Darrell's books traverse multiple genres including cozy mysteries, science-fiction and adventure stories. A proud resident of Melbourne, Australia, Darrell shares his home with his wife and says he owns too many books (as if such a thing were possible!)

His literary journey began with a passion for crafting short stories in his youth, eventually evolving into full-length novels. Among his accolades, "A Toaster on Mars" earned a prestigious spot on the shortlist for the 2017 Russell Prize, showcasing Darrell's unique brand of humour. His novel, "The Firebird Mystery", received commendation from The Children's Book Council of Australia as a Notable book in 2015.

Darrell's Teen Superhero series has garnered widespread acclaim, while his Rosie Ryan books are a series of delightful mysteries set in a distinctly Australian environment. Among the books he's currently working on are a tech-thriller, a time-travel novel, and a mystery book set in 1960's Victoria.

www.ingramcontent.com/pod-product-compliance
Lightning Source LLC
Chambersburg PA
CBHW010341170726
48283CB00009B/2901